THEN A BOY

Sometimes, what is rooted within you...

...was never yours to have to reap.

READER WARNING:

This book contains varying degrees of the following: parental abuse, violence, school related trauma, depression, weight issues, horror, and death.

Consider your wellbeing. Please read safely and responsibly.

Then, A Boy

Copyright © 2022 by Sherman B. Mason

This is a work of fiction. Names, characters, places, and incidents are a product of the author's imagination or are used fictitiously. Any resemblance to actual people, living or dead, or to businesses, companies, events, institutions, or locales is completely coincidental.

Cover art and design by Sherman B. Mason

ISBN: 978-0-578-39947-8

Dedicated to "Braxton". We love you.

Or at least, I do.

THEN A BOY

SHERMAN B. MASON

CHAPTER 1

"All that seems to come to mind is the pain. By the time my mind takes me to memories of the better moments, it's time to flinch. After a while, after the first few times, you start feeling the pain from the inside. You start to truly understand what the act of getting abused consists of. The leather-gripping hand going back according to the desired amount of destruction. The belt rushing forward against the subject, relieving the abuser's stress. Transferring hurt onto you until the present god is satisfied. Until their personal justice is served. Until

THEN, A BOY

all there is left is your realization that you are no worthy of discussion and rationalization, but only of being hit. I am the relief."

//

The moment felt new, but it belonged. Everything had changed in those few seconds. People ran past each other, stumbled over themselves. The look on their faces were stirred together with sadness and confusion. Screams belted through the air as the gunshots rang out. With each blast, a body fell to the ground. Parents held their lifeless children in agony before being slaughtered themselves. Fathers, no more. Mothers, no more. Children, no more.

The smoke bellowed high above the sky, leaving the air chalky and unlivable. Everything felt unstable. Nothing was still enough to focus on. Nothing except her. The old woman stood there staring at me as if discovering me for the first time. Her still frame felt out of place in the chaos, like a statue underwater. I looked back at her waiting for something to make sense. A soft smile brushed over her wrinkled face as the man came up behind her and pulled the trigger.

I woke up with my heart racing. Standing over me was my mother clenching her leather belt. She grabbed me by the arm and dragged me out of bed. I stumbled along behind her trying to gain my balance. My mother shoved me into the bathroom. I looked up, still trying to put together what was going on. The scowl on her face felt uncontrolled. She began to hit me repeatedly with her belt. The leather sent jolts of pain throughout my whole body. Between my screams, I could hear me angrily mention something about the kitchen still being dirty.

As she subsided her wrath, I opened my eyes to a pool of my tears, blood, and saliva on the floor in front of me. I didn't dare move, fearing that an adjustment in posture would be interpreted as a demand for conclusion. My body shook from holding myself up for what seemed like forever. All sound had escaped from the room except my whimpering and the abuser catching her breath from all the efforts. I'm sure she felt a rush from being supremely vindicated while I, on the other hand, have been defeated once again.

A swift glimpse of wind quickly cooled my back as the door opened behind me, followed by my mother's harsh footsteps that grew further and further away. The door slammed shut, and I fully collapsed to the cold, wet tile underneath me. I realized I was still clasping onto the brass metal chair I embraced when I was pushed into the room. My fingers slowly blossomed open as I loosened my unrelenting grip, undamming the hot blood from my shaky palms. I laid there and began to weep.

The emotion possessed my being. I got hotter and hotter. Sadness consumed me. Laying there lowered me deeper into my damp stone well of victimhood. "I'm almost done," I thought to myself. "I only got 3 more years left and then I'll be OK. I'm almost done." Before I could summon another thought, I heard the familiar footsteps rushing toward me.

I sat up and wiped a dirty, trembling hand

across my face as quickly as I could. The door swung open, and my mother dominated over me again, even from a distance. She glared into me from the doorway with a hot evil, seemingly ready to disassemble me even more. "Hurry up and get that mess cleaned up!" she yelled, pointing in the direction of the house's kitchen. Kitchens in the movies were always so big and peaceful. Warm pies and laughter. Ours was more of a dungeon with a stove. She must have never put down her weapon. I could see a slight sway of its shadow on the wall.

I pressed my arms against the ground to peel myself from the floor. Once I was able to stand, I carefully maneuvered through the narrow gap she left for me between her massive body and the door frame, being careful not to touch her. I couldn't help but think she would swing at me one more time. I lightly flinched at just the thought of the belt's sound. Thankfully I was able to pass safely that time.

A pile of dishes laid in front of me in the small sink, as dirty as I was. Some, as broken. I always started with the dishes because they always made the kitchen look the worst. I picked them up from the sink one by one and placed them on the table next to me. Families of roaches scurried from underneath. I ran the water to wash them down the drain. The old faucet spewed water from its base like a sprinkler. The sound it made reminded me of snakes hissing.

I organized the dishes to make the task of washing them a bit easier. The large heavier plates got washed first so they would rest at the bottom of the stack in the cabinet. Organizing them always calmed me for some reason. Maybe it was the feeling of control. It felt good getting something in order. I ran the dingy washrag under the running water while the sink filled. The smell of mildew eventually faded away as the citrus bubbles from the dishwashing liquid took over.

Streams of the watered-down dish soap dove through the water as I squirt in more of the little bit that was left. The dark early morning sky hung over me, teasing me with sleep through the dusty kitchen window. I tried to let the smell of the soap take me away. I pictured what it would be like to live in a whole house that smelled liked that forever. The sink filled and I shut the noisy faucet off. I could hear the slight hum from my mother's television uttering inaudible chatter. Laugh tracks broke up the murmur of dialogue while the burst of illumination protruded through the shadowy corner. My mind fought with the freezing cold water to create the sunshine I pictured in my mind from the orange-scented bubbles. The colors I had created returned back to the grayish world around me.

As I was finishing the last of the dirty dishes, I remembered I still hadn't gotten my homework done from the night before. "Another late assignment," I thought. "I can't keep doing this." I had told my teachers I would start 'trying more' to cover up what was going on at home. I could never figure out why I protected my mother so much after all she does to us. I hated being compared to kids at the school who didn't care. My daydreams of a way out fleeted my mind. I sank my numbed hands in the frigid water hoping it spread all the way through me until the morning.

CHAPTER 2

"It's freezing outside, but the sun is beaming. I never understood that. The sun is so huge and hot. It can change the color of people's skin from millions of miles away. It can make you blind if you even look at it for too long. But also, it can be there and do absolutely nothing at the same time. Makes me think of adults. They can love you and hate you in the same body. It's unfair. They should be called something else when they aren't doing what they are meant to do. Being alive longer should require more from you, not excuse you from more. I have to be everything

*that someone my age is supposed to be with no
exceptions. That's not right. Adults are the sun."*

//

My younger brother Genie stood at the bus
stop seemingly unphased by the weather, as he huffed
into the cold December air. "Hicks!" he shouted at
me. Our family called me that because I used to get
hiccups a lot. Genie always thought it was pretty
funny. I told him he could keep calling me that as
long as he let me call him "Genie" instead of his real
name Eugene.

"What," I replied.

"I'm making clouds!" Genie blurted.

He breathed in as much as his patience
allowed and blew all the air he could from above his
small frame. "See? Clouds." I looked into his
dissipating "clouds" and watched them fade away
until all there was left was his prideful grin. I smiled
at him and looked down the street to see if his bus
was anywhere in sight. It wasn't. "Hicks!" Genie

yelled, piercing my focus. My gaze jolted down at him partially from being startled but also because he was getting on my nerves. Like he did every morning.

"Can I get on your back?" he asked.

"No," I replied coldly.

I was so glad my mother wasn't out there to force me to carry him around.

"Please?" he begged.

"No."

"Why not?"

"Because I don't feel like playin' right now. And your bus is comin' soon."

"I can get on your back for a little bit, and then when my bus comes, I can get back off your back when it's time to get in the bus."

Between Genie's whining, I eventually heard a small hum in the distance. The bus. "Thank God," I murmured under my breath. "What?" Genie said, immediately putting an end to his complaining. I pointed to the toy car-sized bus I saw down the street from us.

"I said 'There's your bus,'" I lied.

"Aw, man!" Genie said, happy to see his friends soon.

He seemed to like school a lot. "Give it time," I thought. I saw the bus slow down and stop a block or so down from us at one of the other stops. I could barely make out the stop sign that protruded from the side until after a couple of stops before us. "That's my friend Nathan!" Genie pointed to the miniature figure with the oversized backpack entering the now larger bus. "I know," I appeased. He told me that every day we were out there. "Yesterday, Nathan said I can come to his house when we are done at school! But mom said 'No.'" said Genie. A twinge of sadness breezed over his face, but the bus pulled up in front of us before it had its full effect.

I could hear the stop sign creek on the other side of the bus as it opened. Blinking red snow pulsed on and off from its one good light. When the door opened, a whisper of warm air brushed over me. It stayed and hovered for a second until the winter wind shooed it away. "Bye!" Genie yelled in the air to me as he ran up the stairs on the bus, abandoning the snow from his boots.

"Well, hi Eugene!" the bus driver said through her practiced smile. She looked up to check her mirror, making sure he ended up sitting down. I heard a couple of kids yell his name in excitement when he got on. It was almost like they don't see him most of the week. The bus driver always looked at me and tried to tell me to have a nice day over the child circus she had to drive around. I usually end up just waving. She shut the door, and the stop sign creaked back in place. The bus made that hissing sound that buses make and pulled past me, seemingly leaving me behind in the dirty snow and frozen rocks. "Until next time, bus," I said.

Then, it was my turn. It always seemed like a race to school for me. I never knew what time it was after I leave the house. I decided that it felt like I walked for at least half an hour before I saw Ashley Street, the cross street my school was on. I always looked for the head of that old, malnourished Viking on top of the school.

THEN, A BOY

My sister Nikki told me someone cut its head off one night back when she was going there. She said the whole school was mayhem that day trying to find out who did it, but no one said anything. I remember wishing I could have seen it when she was telling me the story. If you looked close enough, you could still see the line across the neck from where they had to weld the head back on. I thought of that story every time I saw the statue.

It took me longer to get to school sometimes because of the weather. Most of the sidewalks and backstreets I took were covered in ice. The city workers weren't going to be in my neighborhood, wasting their salt on the roads I used. I walked where the grass seemed to be the last time I had seen it unless that was frozen over too. I hated winter more every time I had to walk in it. I never saw the point of it being that cold and people living there on purpose. I always thought of winter as more of a punishment than a season.

Suddenly as I was walking, sharp pain in my head struck me. I stumbled around as my legs hesitated to cooperate. Somehow managing to stay on my feet, I clenched my eyes shut and squeezed my head with my hands. It didn't help. The pain was worse than the episodes I had had before. I could feel myself starting to get dizzy. Everything began to spin.

My head felt like it was pulsing and was going to explode at any moment. When the nausea started, I swallowed over and over again to keep the vomit from coming up. I slowly opened my eyes to find something to focus on. That helped me once before. A mangled Coors Light box on the side of the road was all I could make out under all the snow. My eyes gripped onto the snow-filled box trying to keep everything still.

It wasn't long before I realized I hadn't been breathing. I pushed out everything I had been holding in, creating a brief fog in front of me. A glimpse of Genie's prideful grin flashed in my mind. I tried to steady my breathing, but the cold air stampeded my teeth and shut my mouth immediately. I attempted again but a little more carefully.

In.

Out.

In.

Out.

My head eased up a bit, and my eyes pried open more and more with each breath. The Coors Light box I fixated on stared back at me, seemingly coaching me through the pain. After a few moments, everything gradually shifted back to normal. I slowly looked around to see if anyone was watching, scared to move too suddenly. No one seemed to care. I widened my eyes and took a slow deep breath.

The head pains I had been hiding were getting worse. And more frequent. I was surprised no one at home had caught me yet. I had to figure out what I was going to do. My legs were frozen solid from me standing still so long, but I managed to eventually make it to the proud Midland Viking. I walked up to the front entrance of the school. The school grounds were a complete ghost town. A sure sign that I was late. The last time I was late was my last strike. I assumed I would be in the Big House the following day. I pushed the door buzzer to be let in.

"Hello, how can I help you?" the tin voice asked.

"I need to g-, I need to get in," I said, voice shaky from the cold.

"And who is 'I'?" the tin voice replied. I knew she could see me on the camera overhead. But every time I was late, she forced me to say my name.

"Braxton Tatum," I belted unwillingly. The door buzzed and unlatched loudly, echoing through the empty air behind me. I pulled myself in and was immediately grateful to be out of the cold. The hallways were quiet and calm. I wished it were like that all the time. It was almost worth being late. I was taking off my beanie when it suddenly hit me: I never finished that stupid assignment. I stuffed the beanie in my pocket wondering what I was going to say to my teachers this time. I fumbled around excuses in my mind, trying to remember what I had said to which teacher already. As my thoughts fell flat, I prepared myself for the worst.

CHAPTER 3

"I wonder what would happen if schools taught you how to think. There should definitely be a thought class. The rest is so pointless. So many kids here can't grasp simple logic, and yet we get to move forward in these grades like a good job was done. But that seems right, I guess. The world relies on people not genuinely thinking about what's going on. No one really cares if the cashier at the store knows Algebra or if the mechanic passed Biology class.

Most of this junk they try to force us to remember seems so irrelevant for life. They hurl exams at us and use the results to categorize us into the proper box. I didn't sign up for or agree to this. No one teaches you how to make things any better. Just how to be good at what they deemed 'good' and obey their instructions. But I guess the fries aren't going to cook themselves."

//

I walked into the class, and everyone looked at me in unison as I came in like they did every time I was late. I slid my tardy slip from the office onto Mr. Fredrickson's desk and walked over to my desk.

"You headed to the Big House, my man!" whispered Morris.

"Shut up," I replied, pulling the book bag off my shoulder. I plopped down in the seat of my desk, relieved to finally be able to sit. He leaned back over towards me carefully. He made sure to keep his eyes locked on the teacher, so he doesn't get caught.

"You da pappy," he whispered.

I looked away and bit my tongue to keep from

laughing. I didn't need any more trouble. Hearing Morris' laugh breaking through his inconspicuous hand gesture made things worse. I managed to somehow keep my mouth shut. I looked up at the teacher, who seemed to be oblivious to how soon he was about to have to kick us out of the class. I didn't dare look over at Morris until I'd gained some sort of composure.

"Ay, I had another one of those things today on the way here," I whispered.

"Aw, man. You gotta get that mess checked out," Morris murmured back, still undetected. We had gotten good at this over the last year.

"Today was the worst one. It's getting bad."

Silence eased between us. Whatever was going on with me was getting worse. I was still a little nauseous, but the dizziness seemed to be gone, for now. I immediately dismissed the thought of going to a hospital. I saw my grandpa die in the hospital when I was younger. I've hated them ever since. I never forgot the screams he belted out for us to keep him safe. Him trying to back away from whatever he saw through his faded milky eyes. The lack of control.

I remembered it being so calm right before. Then all of a sudden, instant chaos. My dad tried to grab my arm and drag me out of the room, but I couldn't turn away. Something about it was so gripping. It was so real to me, seeing fear that close. The look on his seized face will forever be with me. I remember the difference between him being still and him being dead. I could never find the words to describe it. But I knew.

I thought of the pains getting even somehow worse and that being me one day. Old, dependent, and hopeless. I briefly wrestled with each side. "If I got help now, maybe I won't be like my grandpa later." I thought. I didn't ever want to be as scared as he was that day. Ever. But I really didn't want to tell my mom what had been going on. I had never gone to her with any of my problems. Even if I told her, she would minimize it or blame it on me somehow. I couldn't think of a scenario bad enough for her to care.

I snapped back, shaking my head to free myself from my thoughts. I glanced over at Morris, who seemed to have noticed me doing it.

"Yeah, I think you're right," I said through a sigh. "But I'm not tryin' to go to no hospital."

"I feel you," he replied.

Mr. Fredrickson seemed to look in our direction for a second but then went on saying something about someone named Galilei being 68 when he wrote the book he was quoting from.

"My stomach still kinda hurts, though." I did the signature hand-on-stomach thing people do for no reason.

"I know what can fix that," Morris said, slowly looking around him. I looked at him curiously. "The prison hooch." Miraculously, the bell rang right as we burst into laughter in front of everyone. A few eyes looked at us and smiled. The class was used to him and I playing around in there. The only one not amused was Mr. Fredrickson.

"Gentlemen!" He said, raising his voice with every syllable like he did with us every week. "We know, we know," Morris interrupts. "We're leaving." We gathered our things together and headed toward the door. In no hurry, of course. I was never excited about having to part ways for the next class. I really didn't talk much to anybody else at the school besides Morris. I wouldn't see him again until lunchtime.

"I'm so sick of this trash school!" Morris said once we were in the hallway.

"Yeah, for real. We're halfway done, though. 2 more years, and we're good." I flung my heavy bag back over my shoulder.

"You're always counting down days," Morris replied with a laugh.

"That's the only way I keep myself together."

"Yea, that's probably a good idea. We need an advent calendar. Alright man, I'll see you later."

"Bet," I replied.

We do our signature handshake from freshmen year.

"Enjoy your freedom while you got it!" Morris yelled over his shoulder at me. I could hear his maniacal laugh over all the conversations and slamming lockers.

My next class, Geometry, was always a waste of time. Mrs. McGloflen's voice didn't make it any better. She sounded like she needed to swallow all the extra juice in her mouth to talk right. I didn't know why but it really annoyed me. Geometry wasn't going to mean anything in the future anyway. I was doodling in my textbook when I heard the daily intro to the Codependent Comedy Hour in the classroom.

"Ay, dark-shmellow!" Muffled chuckles scattered around behind me. "Hey! How is your back pregnant?" Another voice picked up on the momentum. "Why does the back of his arms look like speed bags?" One of the girls now saw it was safe to chime in. "His arm meat look like Mr. Krab's daughter." Everyone behind me erupted in laughter.

"QUIET!" Mrs. McGloflen squawked. Her juicy voice had no effect. It never did. The laughing continued to roar and spread throughout the class. Character-extinguishing stares smothered me. Heat washed over my whole body. The sound seemed amplified by someone banging their fist on their desk: the ultimate sign that someone thinks something is funny. "QUIET!" Mrs. McGloflen tried again. No avail.

Someone started sparring the back of my right arm, completely ruining the drawing I was doing to distract myself. I moved my arm as my grandest sign of defiance and found somewhere else to draw in my notebook. I could only faintly hear Mrs. McGloflen over the hyenas around me after a while. The class was the victor again.

"They really need to get better teachers in this school," I hissed mentally. "It's already bad enough that we have to sit here most of the day. Then, this." I scribbled out the rest of my destroyed drawing. "It could be worse, I guess. I could be at home." I honed in on my doodles through the duration of the class until I heard the bell ring.

CHAPTER 4

"*People should talk about time more. There's such a lack of emphasis on the fact that this year we're in, this month, this week, this day, this hour, this minute, this second, or this very moment will never be allowed again. In fact, there is no such thing as 'this' moment. It's over before you finish saying it. It's like trying to grab that one grain of sand in the hourglass. By the time you go to reach for it, it's covered, never to be seen directly again. Only remembered.*

Time is our greatest friend but is also the biggest bully. It can heal wounds and nourishes us back to *health but kills you after being in it too long. No one is exempt from its demand since its employer is death itself. The fear in us tries to kill it but we only hurt ourselves as the sand falls from above, covering us in hours that rush past us. It's cruel how it can't be grasped but still slips away. It keeps hidden what lies ahead. Secrets that only <u>it</u> will tell."*

//

I couldn't even look her in the eyes. I tried to stare at something on her desk, but the embarrassment dominated the space I was attempting to create in my head. My hands roamed around my pockets for something to fidget with. Nothing was there. I could feel my forehead start to get hot. The tension from the silence grew louder than any words that could have been spoken. The empty classroom helped me open up.

"I was gonna do the paper like I said I would, bu-"

"But you didn't have *time*?" Mrs.

Cunningham interrupted.

I finally looked up at her. I nodded, letting her believe that that is what I was going to say. She didn't seem mad. She was more disappointed. Which still hurt. It was weird not being yelled at when I messed up, but it was a very welcomed change of pace. I really didn't want to disappoint Mrs. Cunningham, though. She was the only teacher, or I guess the only adult in my life, that made me feel like I meant something.

One day last year, she told me that there was something special about me. That I was different than most kids. She would always seem so blown away at the homework I turned in. She wanted to meet my parents and tell them how advanced she thought I was, but I made up some lie about them being sick. I'm not sure if she believed me but she never came by.

"Braxton, do you remember what you wrote in your assignment earlier this year about the subject of time?" I shook my head. "About how it actually has *us* instead of us having *it*? So we shouldn't 'spend' what isn't ours?" She sat down at her long wooden desk, covered with teacher-looking things. Everything but my assignment. She leaned back in her creaky chair. Her gaze was sturdy and sure. "That *really* intrigued me, Braxton. I've shared your words with numerous people. So why is it that something you wrote can change *me* but not *you*?"

I didn't know what to say without telling the truth. "I was up all night getting beat and cleaning the house? When I got done, I didn't have any light to see what I was doing, and even if I did, I was too tired to focus?" I was sure that wouldn't go over well. Mrs. Cunningham's look went from directness to concern. I realized I had to clean up whatever mess my facial expression had just made.

"Yea, you're right. I just got sidetracked but I know that ain't no excuse. I need to for real stop playing," I said, trying my best to fix the damage. Mrs. Cunningham leaned forward, seemingly searching for something within me. "Braxton…" she said with concern. I immediately slammed the door to her examination. "I'll take a zero for this one," I declared. "I'll try to make up the grade before the end of the quarter."

I looked around the room and landed my gaze on a snowy tree outside, just a few feet from her window. I wasn't sure how good of an actor I was, but I couldn't have her coming to my house or something like that. "Braxton. Listen," Mrs. Cunningham replied, a little sharper, but not harshly. I looked back at her. She seemed to put whatever she was looking for inside me on hold for a moment. "You are one of the brightest kids I know. Hell, I'm sure you're one of the brightest in this *school*. I know you can do the work I give you. I only want you to succeed. That's the only reason I stay on you about this," She sat back again in her chair. "Listen. I can make some arrangements to stay after school tonight to help you. But only this one time."

My mind peeked at the idea but quickly snapped back into my reality. There was no way my mom was going to let me stay after school to do anything when I could be at home cleaning something. Walking home when it was dark out would be so nice. Freezing to death would be worth it. I hadn't seen much of the night before. I always pictured it being so peaceful. So far, I had only the muffled stars through our smudgy bathroom window. Just the thought of walking home under them accidentally slipped a quick smile on my face. I forgot I was supposed to be acting.

Mrs. Cunningham saw my smile as a green light for her plan. "Ok, it's settled," she proclaimed, slamming her palms on her desk with excitement. She stood up to shake my hand. I tried to quickly make something up, but Mrs. Cunningham grabbed my sweaty loose hand from my side and shook it vigorously. She smiled, and I nervously smiled back, wondering how I'm going to get myself out of this mess I had just gotten myself into. I decided to ask Morris at lunch.

"Bruh, where you been?" Morris shouted as I dropped my heavy bag onto the cafeteria floor.

"I got jammed up in Mrs. Cunningham's class," I explained.

"Aw. I like her. She's pretty cool," he replied.

"You better hurry up and jump in line. They got wings today!"

My response seemed to make my tardiness excusable.

I didn't like spicy food much, but I was pretty hungry. I got in line and grabbed some wings, the rock-hard fries they tried to kill us with every day, and a chocolate milk. Morris was almost finished eating by the time I got back to him.

"Lemme get one of them wings, bruh," Morris begged, staring at my food while rubbing his hands and licking his lips. I always wondered how he stayed in shape, eating the way he did. It was pretty frustrating to see.

"Naw, you cartoon!" I replied, pulling the tray closer to me. "Go pretend you somebody else and get some more!"

"Hmm. That's a good one." I could see him contemplate the idea but we both knew it wasn't going to work. He was too funny, and I was sure he said something hilarious when he was in line. He had a way of always bringing attention to himself. He'd be busted in a couple of seconds. "Nah, I'm good," he concluded as he devoured his last hot wing like a garbage disposal. We both laughed at his foolishness.

"Yo, I can't stand this school," I said.

"Yea, I feel you," replied Morris. "We almost in the clear, though."

"I was about to slap somebody in Ms. McGloflen's class," I lied. I was pretty sure Morris knew I was lying, but he played along anyway, for my sake.

"Yea, I heard some dude saying some junk about that class in gym class today. I started roasting his randomized hit-or-miss lost & found teeth. The whole gym was dyin'."

"Lost and found teeth!" We both started laughing so loud, it felt like we interrupted the entire school's conversations.

"Yea, I almost got kicked out," Morris said, wiping the tears from his eyes.

I finished my food and we headed into the courtyard. The wind wasn't as bad there so the cold was easier to handle. Even though there were small crowds of people scattered around, it seemed quieter than inside. The football players were running and sliding from the opposite side of the courtyard to see who could go the farthest. Probably to impress the girls watching from the far-right corner. Others were sitting on the tables along the sides, showing each other videos on their phones. In the left corner, the quiet people were having an unusually loud discussion and reenacting something they must have watched on TV or something. A couple of security guards obliviously stood in the middle, talking with their hands about something that was probably stupid. Morris and I walked over to a lonely table, seemingly put there away from its family against its will.

"Ay, man, so I messed up," I blurted.

"What do you mean?" Morris asked.

"I accidentally told Mrs. Cunningham that I would stay after school to do homework."

Morris sucked his teeth. "Why'd you do *that*, fool?"

"I mean, I didn't really *tell* her, I guess. She

just th-"

"What you mean you didn't tell her?" Morris interrupted, laughing.

"I mean, she thought I… she thought I could," I explained.

"Huh? How?" Morris asked.

"I mean, she suggested it, and I didn't get a chance to say 'No'."

"You already know Gahzella gon' wild out," He replied. "Gahzella" was what Morris called my mom after I told him a story about my sister calling her Godzilla once when she was little.

"Yea, I know. I don't know what I'm gonna do."

A pause entered the conversation as we both tried to think of an exit for my lack of sense.

"I know!" Morris exclaimed. "Why don't you just not show up and say you forgot?"

"Because this all started with me saying I forgot something in the first place. If I tell Mrs. Cunningham I forgot again, she's gonna be even more heated."

"All the teachers leave right after school anyway. She's not gonna stay."

"She said she would make arrangements," I replied.

"Aw, you struck!"

"Yea, I know."

We got quiet again and heard the football players cussing. We looked over to see them shoving each other back and forth. The two guards were already on their way over to them. "Let's get out of here," I said. I couldn't be around violence or people yelling for too long.

We grabbed our book bags and headed towards the exit from the courtyard. People were running past us to get a better view of the altercation. We went in through the exit door, where it was a lot quieter.

"I gotta go to the bathroom," Morris said. "Those wings were a trap."

"Alright, I'll see you after school," I replied.

"Bet."

We did our handshake and parted ways again.

The rest of the school day was a blur. All day, I was trying to figure out how I was going to get myself out of the afterschool thing with Mrs. Cunningham. My mother wanted me home directly after school. If I wasn't home by whatever time it usually took me to walk there, she would be out looking for me. I pretended I didn't see her. She would drive around the blocks she knew I walked down. I always assumed it was to make sure I wasn't smoking crack or getting someone pregnant. When I was about a block or two from the house, she sped back home before I could get there and pretended that she was there the whole time. I could usually smell the old, burning hot engine on my way inside.

The last bell rang for dismissal, and it felt like I was about to die. I was hot all over. I had no plan to save to me. I made my way to Mrs. Cunningham's room, but to my surprise, it was empty. My mind cycled through possibilities of where she could be. *"Maybe she was out looking for me,"* I thought. *"Or maybe my mom snatched her up after she called her about me staying after school."*

A lump in my throat made it hard to swallow. I sat down at my desk in the left corner of the room, grinding my teeth and shaking my leg. I didn't remember ever being that nervous before. I tilted forward to look as far down the hall as I could from my seat, but there was still no sign of her. The sound of excited students leaving school got less and less thunderous with every minute that went by. I was officially scared.

I got up from my desk to go check the hallway and in came Mrs. Cunningham, panting as if she had run there. She was on her phone and looked extremely worried. "Ok. Yes. Ok. Ok. Thanks for calling. Alright. Ok, bye." She took a deep breath and put her cell phone on her desk on top of a stack of papers. "Sorry, Braxton." I opened my mouth to let her know it was okay, but she interrupted my unsaid words.

"We're going to have to reschedule," she panted.

"That's fine," I replied. Fireworks and champagne bottles popping open filled my mind.

Mrs. Cunningham gathered a few things from her desk and began putting them in her messenger bag. "I'll give you another day to get that assignment to me," She said, in haste. "But I don't want any more excuses."

"Ok, yeah. No problem," I confirmed. "I'll get it done."

"Good," she replied.

I made my way out of the room and almost wanted to start singing. I couldn't believe it all worked out. I hoped everything is ok with Mrs. Cunningham, though. All I knew was I wasn't going to get killed that night. I just had to get home before my mom started patrolling the streets.

CHAPTER 5

"I wonder where the sky starts. At what point does the 'air' become the sky? To ants, people are giants. I wonder if we are in the sky to them. Maybe I'm always in the sky, and something like birds or airplanes are just higher up in the same sky. Or maybe, I'm disqualified from being in the sky since I'm always touching the ground in some way. What if we lost our privilege to be in the sky and now have to walk everywhere? Maybe we're all just penalized serpents.

We can't even handle the ground. We have no right to

be in the air with something as free as a bird or clouds. It's almost disrespectful to stand over ants as if we earned it. They continuously work with no sleep and do right by each other without the gift of the sky at all. They'll never fathom what we have. And instead of sharing and working together like them, we step on them on our way to hurt others."

//

The next morning seemed pretty typical. I made Genie some cereal and got him dressed pretty quickly. My mother was asleep, so there was no noise from her. My sister Nikki was gone already. Genie and I went to the bus stop, and I watched him make his clouds until the bus came and I made my way to school. I was able to start some of the late assignment for Mrs. Cunningham the night before but couldn't finish it because the bathroom needed cleaning. I finished what was left on my way to the school. I did pretty well, although it was hard to read, write, and walk at the same time.

I was able to make it to school before being locked out. I walked over to the usual spot I go to when I'm not late and saw Morris talking to some girl. As usual. He noticed me coming up, said something to her, and she walked away. He met me on my way over to him.

"So, I see you ain't dead. You good?" he asked.

"Yea, I'm good. Mrs. Cunningham ended up having an emergency. She told me to just bring in the assignment today," I answered.

"YOU BETTA PRAISE *GOD*!" Morris proclaimed, clapping with each word.

"I couldn't believe it. I still can't."

"Did you get it done?"

"Yea, it's done. Ay, do me a favor." I spun my bag around, unzipped it, and pulled out the assignment. "Could you give this to Mrs. Cunningham today? I'm pretty sure I'm on the Big House List today from being late yesterday."

"Yea, I'll handle it." Morris took the paper from me and put it in his bag.

"Thanks, man," I said.

Sure enough, I got to the school bulletin board, and my name was on the list. "BRAXTON TATTOM" They spelled my name wrong every time, but I had gotten used to it. I went to my locker to grab my Big House essentials. Pen. Notebook. MP3 player with the broken headphone that I put up my sleeve. Rock hard cafeteria granola bars. I made my way through the noisy, obnoxious hallways to get to the Big House.

I walked through the school maze and found myself standing at the infamous Big House. The Big House was what we called in-house suspension at the school. The small window on the door was filthy and cracked in the corner. There was grime covering the wood grain, almost as part of the door at that point. There were signs on both sides of it that read "NO FOOD. NO DRINKS. NO TALKING. NO SLEEPING." Someone scraped out part of the word "NO" from the sign on the right. The corner of the sign had the screw pulled out and was bent as if someone tried to take it off of the wall. Dust from the stripped screw hole in the wall was sprinkled on the floor under the sign where people pushed the screw in and out.

I took a deep breath and tried to enjoy one last moment of freedom for the day. I turned the loose, broken knob and pushed my way in. All eyes raced toward me as I entered. That reaction was getting old. I recognized a few faces, but none I really cared about. I quietly shut the door behind me and stood next to the desk in the front.

The desk in the room was nothing like Mrs. Cunningham's desk. There was a tattered calendar and old Post-It notes under a thick sheet of glass layered over the whole top of the desk. A bunch of sticky-looking coffee mug rings were scattered all over. It had an old computer monitor and a yellowing keyboard in the center. Mr. Pallagerski was in his big office chair reading his newspaper and didn't turn to look at me at all.

"I'm supposed to be in here today," I said to Mr. Pallagerski.

"There ain't no food in here, fam," one of the

inmates replied. The audience laughed. There was a guy on the right side of the room whose laugh sounded like a duck.

"Enough!" Mr. Pallagerski yelled. The laughter was brought to a simmer. "What's your name?"

I hesitated for a second until I realized he was speaking to me. "I'm Braxton Tatum," I responded.

Mr. Pallagerski sucked his teeth at the duck boy, who looked back in our direction and snuffed out the rest of his laughter. He lowered his newspaper, being very careful to keep his place in the article he was reading. "Cell phone," he ordered coldly. He tickled his hip until he felt his keychain clip, found his desk key, and unlocked his desk to reveal a plastic bucket with several cell phones in it. The smell of basements and marijuana came toward me as the drawer opened. "I don't have a phone," I said. He looked up at me quickly, ready to snap but then realized that I was that one kid he saw from time to time that actually didn't have a phone.

He slammed the drawer shut, almost as if he

was disappointed in me. "Have a seat," he said, marking my name as being present on his attendance sheet. I looked around for an empty booth. Nothing seemed appealing. The one next to the duck boy was open, but he smelled like weed. I studied the seat next to a girl in the corner closest to the narrow blurry glass window. I headed that way and started to take the bag from my shoulder until I caught her glare. She softly shook her head. I decided to sit at the desk across from her.

"My mom should be in here dealing with this. I'm not the reason I'm always late," I speculated to myself. After a quick grumble or two and some obvious objection to my seating choice, the room returned to the silence I found it in. The booth I was in was filthy. There were crumbs brushed back up against the flimsy fabric-covered panel in front of me. Someone attempted to scrub out the "If u wanna gud time call yur mom" written in permanent marker on it. Gang carvings decorated the wooden desk. I knew looking at that spelling all day was going to drive me nuts.

I opened up my bag and grabbed the pen and notebook I got from my locker earlier. I turned the pages until I got to the drawing that I started the last time I was in there. Mr. Pallagerski seemed to be still inquiring about whatever he was reading in his newspaper. While he was distracted, I eased my earbud tucked through my left sleeve up to my ear and slowly reached toward my pocket where my mp3 player was. I tapped the play button through my pocket, which I had become an expert at.

The hours passed slowly. They intentionally didn't put a clock in the room, but if you listened closely, you could faintly hear the bells ring. If you missed one, you'd have to wait until lunch to see how long it had been. A few people were antsy, but most of the others seemed like repeat offenders. I had to admit, it was getting pretty old being banished to The Big House all day. But I couldn't help being late. I hated being in class, but The Big House had its own problems. I had no clue how the people that weren't smuggling music in were getting through it. I had gotten the "battery low" warning twice already. So, I was going to find out soon.

Suddenly, Mr. Pallagerski's watch alarm went off. Lunchtime. The few newbies looked around, trying to figure out what the sound was. "Alright, line up," Mr. Pallagerski said. We launched out of our chairs. The sound of groans and yawning filled the room. There were some murmurs and a couple of guys trying to inconspicuously hit each other. I made out a few whispers here and there from the new kids trying to find out what was going on. We all lined up, facing the door. Mr. Pallagerski briefly looked up and down the booths to make sure no one was sleeping. He cleared his throat to prepare for his prepared daily speech.

"Alright, ladies and gentlemen," he began in his usual haughty voice. "This is what I like to call 'The Privilege of Eating.' You are going to follow me to the cafeteria where you will be presented with two options. Peanut butter & jelly sandwiches or a salad." Profanities and mumbling were heard in front and behind me. "Is there a problem?" Mr. Pallagerski challenged. Silence ensued.

"While you are down there," he continued, "the same rules apply. There will be no talking and no sleeping. And there will be absolutely no interaction with other students you see in the hallway. You will get your Privilege, and you will sit *down*. If you are unable to appreciate your Privilege by following these rules, it will be thrown away, and you will remain hungry and hopeless. Are there any questions?"

No one spoke out. "Good. Follow me." The door swung open, and the fresh glance of the real world reminded me that time in The Big House wasn't forever. We marched down the quiet halls like sky-less ants following orders. I saw one of the guys tag someone in front of him. The new "it" swiped behind himself but couldn't reach his playmate without turning around, so he just flicked him off and kept walking.

We eventually made it to the cafeteria. It was always odd seeing it completely empty. The area was partially trashed from the lunch hour before. They always brought the Big House kids in after the real lunch break to help make the experience worse. We went over to the cart with the food set out for us. I grabbed a peanut butter & jelly sandwich and sat at one of the designated tables by myself.

I daydreamed in the direction of the cart full of salads. Thoughts would come and then gently float away. I looked up at the cafeteria clock. 7 minutes left. I was grateful I was halfway through the day. Although getting out of that room was ok for a while, it was already getting old just sitting in the cafeteria. It felt odd that it was so quiet.

All of a sudden, I felt light-headed again. The familiar wave of nausea rushed against me. "No, no, no, no, no. Not here," I begged from myself. The room started to spin faster than I had ever experienced before. I tried to get up, but I couldn't stand. I unclenched my eyes to find something to focus on. Everything flew past my vision. I lost anything I tried to lock my eyes on. Things began to blend together as they blurred into everything else.

The sound of shuffling chairs and gasps made me panic. I couldn't make out anywhere they were coming from. I felt cold inside. The feeling was new and confusing. I didn't have time to focus on it for too long before I crashed into a table in front of me. I noticed what had to of been Mr. Pallagerski coming toward me. Stumbling through the debris of my mind's hurricane to get to him, I reached forward. But I was too late. The table rushed towards me. Everything turned black.

CHAPTER 6

"The time has come," she said softly.

"Adherence."

"Meaning."

55

"Elation."

"Tranquility."

57

"Choose."

"Meaning," I chose.

"And so, it is," she replied.

CHAPTER 7

"Friendship is an odd idea. The intertwining of lives based on the rarity of connection. There is nothing special about friendship besides the fact that we choose to hate someone less. Even the worst of people could claim to be friends with someone. I wonder if we are actually friends with people or are we just friends with what they have to give. Is there a limit to what can be gained from people? Do we eventually get to the point where nothing further can be offered from anyone? Is that 'loneliness'? What is a person empty of offers?"

//

My eyes slowly broke open. The light was white and blinding. Slow, soft beeping could be heard to my immediate right. I tried to lift my head but felt as if I was kept still by a weighted mind. The pain in my arm burned. My curiosity eventually revealed itself as worry. I forced my eyes open even more. Murmurs and footsteps were in the distance, but I couldn't make out what was being said or where it was coming from.

I had hoped I wasn't where I thought I was, but it was becoming clearer with each moment. A sinking feeling pressured my stomach to vomit. My heartbeat picked up. I started to sweat. Broken breaths expelled from me as I tried to get up from the hospital bed. "No. Please, no," I said. An arm grabbed me. I pulled away as hard as I could. "Get me out of here!" I shouted. "Get me out of here *now*!"

My panic turned to rage as the carrousel of

emotions inside me continued to spin. More footsteps rushed toward me. I fought with every ounce of strength in me. Voices around me called my name, telling me to calm down. That everything was ok. I ignored them all. I screamed as the force against me pressed me down into the bed. I grew tired. My headache began to get a lot worse. I stopped and fell still in the bed. My surrender brought tears to my eyes. I laid back, begging to be let go.

Soon after, the hospital nurses slowly released my arms. I tried to catch my breath the best I could. Tears drained into my ears. I felt dizzy. Unstable. The voices around me went in and out of focus. I tried to compile my thoughts, but nothing was solid enough to hold on to. I gathered what little energy seemed available in me to turn toward the voices I heard. I was empty. I finally was able to drag my gaze over and saw someone that made me feel more centered. Morris.

"Yo, you good, bruh?" Morris said. The look of concern on his face was something I had never seen on him before. I tried to achieve a reply, but I couldn't find the words to say. The last moments I remembered seemed like drawings in a notepad my mind etched into me. Glimpses of moments that didn't seem to fit together. But embodied their own separate existence.

"What happened?" I finally managed to ask. "Who brought me here?"

"I haven't heard the whole story yet," Morris replied.

"I need to get out of here," I said.

"Let them see what happened first. Just so you-"

"No!" I interrupted. "I can't be here,"

One of the nurses chimed in from the other side of the bed I was in. "Braxton, you aren't going anywhere until we figure out what has been going on." Rage filled me before I knew what to do with it. "Braxton, chill," Morris said. I glared back at him. "Don't tell me to 'chill'. Tell her to mind her damn business!" I turned back to her as she was exiting the room.

"Did you have another one of those things?"

Morris asked when the room was finally empty. "I wanted to tell them about those, but I know you were trying to keep it low key. I'm really worried about you, man." I rested my head back on the pillow and tried to think about the last thing I fully remembered. Then it finally clicked to me that I didn't know why Morris was even there. "How'd *you* get here? I have no clue about what's going on," I said.

"During 5th hour, we all seen an ambulance outside, so we were at the window tryin' to see what was goin' on." Morris paused briefly. I heard him take a deep breath. He continued but in a slightly more wavering voice. "Then I saw it was you," he said. I saw him wipe his face out of the corner of my eye, but I didn't want to look over at him. "I ran after the ambulance right when it started to drive away. When they finally stopped, I told them I was your older brother and we had to stay together. So, they let me come here with you."

The gravity of his sacrifice pressed me inwards. He had always looked out for me, but never like this before. It was nice knowing I was cared for by anyone. It wasn't common for me. It almost brought tears back to my eyes, but I kept myself together for the time being. "Whatchu mean *'older'* brother?" I asked jokingly. The laughing hurt my head but was helpful to us both.

The sound of high heels approached the door and made its way inside the hospital room. "Oh, my goodness! You're awake!" Mrs. Cunningham raced to the side of the bed next to Morris. "He's awake! I'm going to go. Yes. Yes, he is. I will. Alright. Thanks. Bye." She dropped her phone in the pocket of her long black trench coat.

"How are you feeling?" She asked. Her eyes were watery and involved.

"My head hurts. And I feel kinda weak. But I'm ok," I replied.

"Mr. Pallagerski said you didn't look too well before you hit your head," she said. "Are you sure you're alright?"

"Yea. Yea, I'm fine. Can I go? I don't like it here."

She looked at me as if she was going to

question me further but took a deep breath, and let it go. She peered over at Morris, who immediately directed his attention to her, waiting to be chastised. But nothing happened. She glanced at the heart rate monitor near my bed and then looked back at me. "I'm going to go ask the doctor how soon we can get you released." Mrs. Cunningham walked back out of the room. She seemingly more relieved after hearing my status, but wasn't fully sure.

"Yo, I thought she was about to cuss me clean out," Morris said when the coast is clear.

"Me too," I agreed.

After a few moments, Mrs. Cunningham came back into the room with one of the doctors. "Hi!" he said with a smile. "I'm Dr. Coleman." He was a very tall thin man with slicked-back black hair and perfect teeth. His skin was tanned but not orange like the celebrities on TV. I couldn't help but notice his super expensive-looking ring as he was holding a clipboard with the hospital name and logo on the back of it.

"Hi," I replied soberly, curious about what he

was about to tell me. I hoped he would tell me I could go. I didn't want to be there a minute longer than I had to be. But I was still a little too woozy to object at the moment.

"Looks like you had a pretty bad fall," Dr. Coleman said.

I nodded in agreement.

"What do you think caused you to fall?" He asked, searchingly.

"I'm not exactly sure," I said.

"Hmm," he murmured, tapping his pen on the clipboard. His suspension and lack of urgency to get me out of the hospital was starting to bother me. He lifted a page up on his clipboard.

"I think more is going on than what you're saying," Dr. Coleman said. "What were you doing?"

"I was just *sitting* there," I barked.

"Sitting *where*?" he asked.

"School! Where else would I be in the middle of the day? I'm 15!"

The doctor's gaze looked narrower into me. He peeked down at my arms and legs.

"Have you been having odd thoughts at all? Loss of emotion?" Dr. Coleman asked.

"No," I spat coldly.

"Have you been hungrier than usual?

"No."

"Unwarranted anger?"

"No."

Mrs. Cunningham stepped closer to the bed. "Braxton, he's just trying to -"

"I know! I'm fine!" I growled, growing even more impatient. I detached my eyes from Dr. Coleman and looked over at Mrs. Cunningham. "Can we just go?"

Mrs. Cunningham huffed through her nose and looked at the doctor. "Doctor, thank you for all your help today," she said. "I think he just got a little dizzy and fell. Other than that, he seems fine." I looked over at the doctor to see if he agreed. He didn't seem to. He looked at me in disappointment. His scowl was harsh but I was sure mine was just as bad.

He shoved his clipboard and another pen he

had in the pocket of his white jacket toward Mrs. Cunningham. "Sign this release form, and go," he said. His jacket breezed up and ran after him as he headed to the hospital room door. "Oh, and doctor?" Mrs. Cunningham turned toward him. "We'll need a wheelchair to get him to my car." The doctor changed his stare from her to me, then continues his walk out of the room.

Mrs. Cunningham lifted her eyebrows and rolled her eyes up and over. "Nice guy," she muttered. She signed the form then put the clipboard and pen on the counter behind her. "Ok," she said. "We're leaving. Do you think you can get in the wheelchair on your own?" I nodded. Almost arguing with the doctor made me realize I'm a little more energetic than I thought it was.

"C'mon Morris," She said as she walked over to the door and held it open. Morris softly punched me in the arm and followed Mrs. Cunningham into the halls of the hospital. "We're just going to go pull the car up closer to the entrance. I'll be right back to come get you," she said as the shutting door interrupted her.

I scooted over to the edge of the bed. I grunted with every movement. It seemed like I was laying in the hospital bed for longer than I originally thought. I felt a bit lightheaded still, but I felt like I could make it. I sat there for a second to make sure I could get myself together. Right when I decided to stand, Morris burst back into the room. "I gotta pee before we go, or her car is a *wrap*!" he said as he pushed into the room's bathroom.

I got up, but then the nauseousness instantly rushed back to me. The pain in my stomach knocked the wind out of me. My head began to pulse. Then, the sound of rushing waves filled the atmosphere around me. Like I was in the middle of stormy ocean. I looked around to see where it was coming from. I couldn't find the source, but it rose louder and louder until the noise consumed everything around me. My body felt as if it was underwater.

Suddenly, my belly started to fill up like something undammed inside me. The moment of the liquid startled me at first, but I began to somehow feel at peace as the waves washed over me. My eyes tented into a shade of blue I had never seen before. My nauseous and pain faded away. The mysterious water completely engulfed inside of me, coating me with strength. I felt something I have never felt before in my life. Power.

Before I could examine the feeling for too long, Dr. Coleman came through the hospital room door. As soon as he saw me, he aggressively shoved the wheelchair across the room. The look on his face was full of fury. "Finally!" Dr. Coleman spewed sharply. His voice sounded completely different than before. His eyes quickly enlarged and shifted into a wicked shape that no human could ever pull off. His demonic glare didn't lose track of me. The gleam from the saliva that began to run down his chin shined in the bright lights.

Then his body jerked violently repeatedly, and his breathing became heavier and heavier. Small puffs of disgusting-smelling smoke came from his mouth and nostrils drifted into the air just above him. Dr. Coleman, or what *used* to be Dr. Coleman, licked his hungry lips, and cocked his head to angle one eye towards me. "You're a mere *child*," he said. "You aren't worthy enough to carry such power." Dr. Coleman slowly approached me. All of a sudden, he jerked his bobbing head upright and with a wolf-like grin, something in a weird language.

He looked me up and down, scanning my frame completely. I felt his gaze enter me and violate my existence. He jabbed his finger toward me, pointing at me and rambling in a speech that made my skin crawl. Suddenly, the weird water rose up in me. I felt a gap of fear between me and the monster.

Dr. Coleman slowly eased towards me. I felt a readiness that seemed foreign to me but welcomed. Power raced through me like electricity. I moved closer to Dr. Coleman. He leaned back, and his eyes, although still evil-looking, became fearful. Dr. Coleman recoiled back into his original human-like appearance. He wiped his mouth and ran out of the hospital room but not before giving me one last look. A look filled with a readiness for vengeance.

The water I felt inside faded within me. I kept

an eye on the door, waiting for Dr. Coleman to rush back in to attack. Morris burst out of the bathroom with the front of his pants soaked in pee. "What in the *devil* is going on out here?" he yelled at the top of his lungs, grabbing his head with his hands. "Come on! Let's go!" I yelled back.

I took the wheelchair and let Morris sit down, as he was seeming in shock. I snatched open the door of the hospital room and pushed Morris out of the room toward the directions of the elevator signs. I turned left from the nurse's station and seen the big silver elevator doors in front of us. I went over and pushed the elevator door button frantically until the doors open. I pushed Morris inside, who still had his hands on his head in disbelief and pressed the lobby button until the doors shut.

I leaned up against the back wall of the elevator. Closing my eyes and shaking my head, I pant the whole way down. When I opened my eyes again, I saw Morris was still in shock, so I knew the whole ordeal wasn't some sort of medication-induced dream.

"Bruh," He said.

"Yea, I know," I said, even though I didn't know *anything*.

"Bruh."

"Yea, I know."

"Bruh!"

"I know!"

We finally made it to the lobby. I grabbed the handles of the wheelchair and ran as fast as I could toward the exit. The lobby's automatic doors couldn't open soon enough, so I accidentally blasted Morris into the door. He doesn't say a word. We get into the corridor. I stopped for a minute when I saw Mrs. Cunningham getting out of her car, heading back in the hospital to get me from my room. She seemed to not be paying attention.

"Morris!" I hissed.

"Huh?" he replied in a daze.

"Morris!" I repeatedly slapped him lightly on the cheek.

"What, what, what?" he said.

"We can't mention *any* of this to her right

now!"

"Any of *what*? I'm still trying to figure out what I heard!"

"Keep it that way," I said. "For now."

We made our way out of the hospital corridor. Mrs. Cunningham stretched her neck forward to make sure it was really the two of us coming toward her. "What are you doing?" she asked, looking at Morris in my wheelchair covered in urine with me pushing him. I couldn't think of a lie fast enough. She tightened her lips. "Actually, nevermind," she concluded, seemingly trying to just end this night as quickly as we were.

Morris got out of the chair and into the back seat of Mrs. Cunningham's car. I got in the front, put my seat belt on, and started to try to wrap my head around what had just gone down. Abandoning the wheelchair outside, she pulled away from the building. I looked back to see if Dr. Coleman was following us or watching. The lonely wheelchair sat stiff, collecting the flurries from the night sky.

The light sound of talk radio kept us from

sitting in silence until we made it to my house. "Thanks, Mrs. Cunningham," I said, pushing open the car door. She gave me a gentle smile. "Do you need me to talk to you mom?" she asked. I softly shook my head, know it would do no good. "Ok. Bye, Braxton," she replied. "Get some rest.".

I looked back at Morris, who still didn't know what to do with his thoughts. "Alright, man," I say. "Alright," he said without even looking up at me. I shut the car door and watched them pull away into the night. The red taillights coloring the snow reminded me that I was getting home later than usual, so I decided to take my time getting in. I looked up. Stars. I smiled and took a moment to look around. I tried to make out the constellations I had read about before. The huge streetlight overhead was keeping them from me. Then, I heard the door to the house creak open, breaking up the peace like thin winter ice. "Boy!" My mom yelled. I camouflaged a soft sigh with my breath in the cold night air. I walked up to the door, and she snatched me inside.

CHAPTER

8

"I wonder what the first person that yelled felt like inside when they did it. I wonder if they were scared of what just burst out from within them. I wonder what they were yelling about. I would love to see the heat from their eyes as they realized what they could get accomplished by simply saying the same words in a louder voice.

The person yelling insults with their tone, as well. Their volume communicates that they think you are unable to understand them when they are speaking to you in a rational manner. I think part of it is them being mad that you got them to that level of anger. It's such a vulnerable state. Embarrassing. It's so raw and primal. Not in a good way. They're going backward. It's a dominant tantrum. An attacking pout."

//

"Where the hell have you been?" my mother yelled into me. She was gritting her teeth and piercing me with her gaze as usual, but something was different. Her eyes resembled sadness. She was breathing heavier than normal. Her nose was running at some point. For the first time I had ever seen, she looked like she had been crying.

"I had to go to-," I started, with no success.

"Speak up!"

I carefully lifted my voice. "I had to go to the hospital."

"The *hospital*?" Her voice slightly tapered down. Only slightly.

"I passed out and hit my head at school."

She immediately stepped forward and hit me in the face. I squinted my eyes at the twinge of pain I felt in my head. Pulling up my coat sleeve, I showed her the hospital band still on my wrist. My mom grabbed my wrist and snatched me closer to her. She examined the band using the light shining from the kitchen behind her, then, threw my arm back down to my side.

"You don't have enough sense to call?" She belted out.

"They tried to but they - they said the phone was off,"

"You should of said to come by here!"

I knew she heard me say I was knocked out. I silently gave her time to let her figure out how dumb that was to say. But I knew she never would. I started to look down, then see Genie's shadow dart away from the doorway. I didn't want to bring any attention to him, so I looked back at my mother.

Her lip was quivering, and she must've seen me notice because she granted me freedom from the confrontation with only one more hit in the face and stormed out of the living room. "Next time, you better tell them to find me," she said as she headed toward her bedroom.

I picked up my bag from the living room floor and headed toward my room to process what happened. My older sister Nikki opened the door to the bedroom she was in near the living room. Her tall slim frame looked down at me, almost auditing. "You good?" she asked, chewing her gum a little slower. I nodded and walked past her, into the room Genie and I shared. I threw my bag onto my bed. Genie came running at me with widened eyes and opened mouth.

"You was in the hospital?" he said in utter shock.

"Yea," I replied.

"What happened to you?"

"I fell and bumped my head."

"Did you have a cuh-cousin?" He'd obviously been watching too much of something.

"I'm okay, Genie. You need to go to bed."

"You can't go to sleep if you had a cuh-cousin."

"Genie, I'm fine."

"Mom was crying."

"I'm okay. Go to bed."

Genie climbed the latter of the bunk bed to his bed on the top, yawning on the way up. "I drew a Red Ranger today!"

"I'll look at it tomorrow."

He curled up, and I pulled his blankets over him. "It's the red one," he said, turning his back against the dim hallway light. I sat on my bed on the lower bunk. I tried to put together some thoughts about what happened at the hospital. Part of me wanted to be asleep in the Big House. I also kind of still hung on to the thought that I was hallucinating, drugged up on something at the hospital. The night seemed like it was going to be a long one for me. Sleep was nowhere in sight. There was no way I could sleep after what I had seen.

I was lying there trying to make sense of everything when I heard a light tap on the door frame of the room. "Hicks." I looked up and saw the silhouette of my sister. She had just finished her fall semester of college not too long ago. She said she's going to stay at our mother's house for a few days so she could see Genie and I. Afterwards, she was going to a friend's house. She didn't want to deal with the drama at her dad's girlfriend's house. She was better than me. I would have slept in a dumpster before coming anywhere near our mother or the house. But it was good to see her. She seemed to have some worry in her voice.

"I'm going to bed," she said. "I'm just makin' sure you don't need anything."

"Nah, I'm good. Thanks," I replied.

Nikki lingered at the door longer than expected like she wanted to say something else. I answered the question I knew she was going to ask. "I'm fine." It didn't seem to do the trick.

"So, what happened to you, anyways?" She asked.

"I passed out," I replied. "I guess I hit my head when I fell."

"Dang, dummy. You couldn't fall out somewhere safe?"

"Shut it up. I was serving time, so I was tired and couldn't think straight."

"The tardies?"

"Yea."

"I wish I could wait for the bus with him still."

"It's cool. Whatever."

A silence came between us as Nikki seemingly thought of what to say next. Then, when she realized that I hadn't been too clear about what happened, she questioned further.

"What made you pass out? Did you eat that day?" she asked.

"Yea, I had just finished eating," I replied.

I hesitated for a moment, but I had always been pretty open with Nikki. She's the only one I had been able to speak to in my family. I sat up on the bed and looked in the direction of her shadowy figure.

"I've been having these really weird... things," I said.

She straightened up.

"What *kind* of things?" Nikki asked.

"I've been getting really lightheaded and dizzy. I get nauseous. The worst part is the head pain. It feels like someone is stabbin' me in the brain."

"Oh, wow," Nikki said. "That's messed up! Why didn't you-" She stopped herself, answering her question before asking it. "How long has it been goin' on?"

"I can't remember. A while," I said. "They started happening more and more lately. And getting worse and worse every time. The one earlier today was the worse one."

I felt like I said enough, but I kept going. The words oozed out before I could stop them.

"Something super wild happened at the hospital when I was there."

"Oh! What was it?" She quickly looked behind her. "Ay, come to my room, so we don't get caught."

We crept to her room, like old times, making sure to not make any sudden movements to disturb our mother. We peered through the dark to the other side of the kitchen toward our mother's rooms. Her light was off, so we knew we would be good for the rest of the night. Nikki turned off the hallway light. The old bulb above us buzzed and slowly faded to darkness.

We tiptoed into her room. We had learned precisely where to step through the house to be absolutely silent, even with my size. That came in handy when we would sneak into the kitchen to steal food sometimes from the cabinets. We used to practice during the summer when we were younger, and our mom was at work. My sister would call it "Street Rat Boot Camp." It definitely paid off many times.

We turned her light off to make it seemed like she was in her room asleep. The gentle glow from the streetlight that reflected off the white snow softly illuminated her room through her drapes just enough for us to be able to barely see each other. She sat on her bed with her back against the lopsided wooden headboard. I sat in the middle facing her with an ear toward the door to listen for our mother.

"So, what did you see at the hospital?" Nikki

asked eagerly. I realized I sounded more reasonable earlier than I was trying to. She probably thought I was going to tell her about someone that I saw with an arm missing or a lady that had quintuplets. I wished that was all it was.

I began to tell her everything. Everything. About the water stuff. The doctor. Morris peeing on himself. To my surprise, she wasn't calling me crazy. Or laughing at me. She looked scared. More than scared. She was terrified. I hadn't had much time to think it through properly. I started to think that maybe it *was* scarier than I was letting it be. Perhaps I was supposed to be more afraid. Nikki was like a statue on her bed in disbelief. After my story, she was just sitting there, motionless with her hand over her mouth.

"Nikki?" I murmured. "You're getting me spooked. Say somethin'." I looked a little closer and realized she was starting to cry. She slowly lowered her hand, and her tears looked like streaks of glass skin flowing down her face in the light's reflection. She started trying to say something but couldn't seem to get it out. "What is it? Spit it out!" I said, nervously.

"I have to tell you something," she managed. I heard the shaking of her body ruffle her tattered comforter. I didn't interrupt her and let her try to continue. "When you were little, I did somethin'. Somethin' stupid, and I never did anything like that again. Not once."

"What was it?" I replied curiously. She sat up and took a deep breath to prepare herself for what she was about to say. I had never seen her this way before. I knew whatever it was trouble her. A lot. Even in the dimmed lights, I could tell she was getting emotional. I didn't want to press her too hard, but she was starting to get me worried. After a couple of moments, she began to tell me what was bothering her.

"I used to know this girl a long time ago. Her name was Melody. Melody Claypool. I met her Freshmen year at Midland High. She was a Junior. One of the first friends I had when I got there. She was weird. But funny. I liked her a lot. We would skip class to talk and stuff. We were talkin' one day, and she said somethin' about this shop she heard about. It had stuff in it that she wanted to show me." Nikki ground her hands together, nervously staring off as if she was explaining a forbidden movie to me that she had seen in her head.

"I told her I couldn't go because of how mom was about us going places and how I had to watch you. You were still just a baby. Almost a year old around the time. A few days later at school, she showed me a book she got from there. She couldn't stop lookin' through it. I don't like readin', but she got me excited. I wanted to see what she was talkin' about. She said she would let me borrow it when she was done readin' it."

"One time when I knew mom and my dad would be gone all day, I told Melody to come by the house. She came and brought like three of her friends with her. I didn't know them, but I trusted her, I guess. I was kinda scared. But I knew we wouldn't get caught. They were all talkin' about the shop Melody was tellin' me about."

"She told me before she would buy me some stuff from there and I forgot she said that until she handed me a bag. There was a few things in it but she was most excited about a crazy lookin' fruit or somethin' she brought. I'd never seen anything like it before. It was really pretty. I asked if I could eat some, but they told me to wait. Melody and her friends started talkin' to me a million miles an hour about the three owners of the shop. They seemed to like them a lot."

Nikki started to cry again, covering her face in shame. I looked away to give her as much privacy as I could. I was trying to think of why she would be telling me this. Why she was so devastated. I waited a moment for her to gather herself again before saying anything. "Did you finally read the book?" I asked. Nikki very slowly nodded, seemingly remorseful. She lifted her head and looked at me so sadly, my heart burned. "Yea, I read it," Nikki said through a deep hollow breath. She seemed like she was ready to continue.

"After we talked for a while, we came in here

and sat on the floor." I glanced over at her stained carpet covered with an old thick circle rug. "You fell asleep, so I laid you on my bed. I thought we were gonna just keep talkin', but Melody pulled out the book. I'll never forget the look she had on her face."

Nikki shook her head to soften the image in her mind. I could tell it scared her. "I remember hoping she was kidding around. I don't think she was. I don't know. All I know is she wanted me to finally read it. I can remember how heavy it was in my hand. There were a lot of weird pictures and words I didn't understand. There were a lot of instructions too. It didn't make any sense. And it felt funny. It was really weird. Something about it wasn't right. I knew I shouldn't have. But I kept turning the pages."

"Then out of nowhere, you burst into tears from your sleep. So loud. You were crying harder than you ever did before. I remember handing the book to one of them and getting up to get you off the bed. I started bouncin' you to get you to be quiet, but you kept screaming, so I sat back down with them and held you."

"Melody started tellin' me about how the store owners taught her to do the spell with the fruit together with friends because it's supposed to bring some kind of bond or somethin'. It sounded fake, but they were all excited to try it, so I said I was down. She took the fruit out of the bag and put it in the crease of the book. She made sure she was on a specific page. Everybody had to hold up our hands like we were offering something to someone. So, I set you down in front of me..."

Nikki hesitated for a second and blinked away new tears. "I set you down in front of me to do what Melody said. She told us we had to repeat the words on the page together with our eyes closed. She had it memorized, so we repeated after her. We just kept sayin' it and sayin' it. I was so scared. I started to get a really bad feeling in my stomach. I opened my eyes to see if any of the chanting was doin' anything or not. That's when I had seen you gnawing on the fruit."

My eyes widened. I looked away to hide my shock, but I was sure my reaction was apparent.

"What does that mean?" I thought to myself. I wanted to ask what they were saying, but I saw that Nikki was going through enough as it was. *"But it was my life! I was the one that has monsters or whatever trying to kill them."* I thought. Anger began to grow inside me as I thought more about what happened. I tried to figure out why there was no one there to help me. Or why she didn't kick the random people out of the house. Heated questions seared my mind when I heard Nikki continue recounting her story.

"I remember pulling you back in front of me and you dropping the fruit back on the book. I snatched you away pretty hard, so you got scared and started cryin' again. And then he came in." Nikki said. I got chills all over my body at how serious she looked. Everything in me tuned in to her. At first, I thought she meant her dad, but by the look on her face, it definitely wasn't anything ordinary.

Nikki's gaze intensified on me. "I don't want to describe it, but it seemed like it would be a man. At least that's what I called it in my thoughts. I thought maybe they brought someone else with them that got there late or somethin', but they were as scared as I was. Everyone but Melody. She had a weird look as if she was happy to see him. Mesmerized. And he was glad to be there."

I could tell this is something my sister hadn't figured out either. I let her continue. "He kneeled down in the circle and grabbed the fruit from the open book. My body got cold. And numb." Nikki rubbed her arms to remind herself that she was still there with me.

"Then he bit into it. We all watched him." Her mouth seemed to dry up as she resurfaced more and more of that day. But neither one of us budged. "The more he chewed, the more he seemed disappointed. He looked at the inside of it and then at us. Then he spit it out on the floor. He was *pissed*. Melody's face change. She got worried. The man threw the fruit down, and it vanished before it hit the ground. Then he disappeared too."

Nikki leaned against the headboard, looking away from me. I started to think I couldn't take much more of the story. Then she hit me with a final blow that fit all this together and connected everything back to me. "Melody said that he just told her something about coming back to find out which one of us it was."

"Which one of you did *what*?" I hissed at her from fear.

"I don't *know*!" she replied. She had a hushed frustration in her tone. She pounded her fist in her lap. "I don't know!" she said. "None of the rest of us heard anything, and we were all in there together!"

That sent Nikki into a deep sorrow. She started weeping, and I slid down closer to her on the bed. I reached over and placed my hand on her shoulder. She put her hand on my wrist and tried to look up but couldn't seem to manage. "I'm sorry!" she wept. "I'm so sorry!"

I didn't know what to do with all this. I had woken up that morning thinking the day was going to be just another dull day in The Big House. Nikki put her palms over each of her eyes, looking upward for a while, then finally took an anguished breath. "What the hell did I do?" she said under her breath. She put her arms down and looked into me. She looked as though she felt sorry for me. Her eyes were empty and full of regret. I didn't know what to do.

CHAPTER 9

"I remember a time Genie asked me if monsters were real. I started to say 'no', but I like being honest with him. I had to ask myself the same question. When I was his age, I would see monsters in movies or on television and know they were fake. But are they? Why is it that every beast, alien, or creature conjured up for us to watch looks like us?

There are always traits that make them relate to us. Two feet. Two legs. A torso. Two arms. A mouth. Teeth. Eyes. Is it the pride of humans who want to have everything revolve around themselves? Do we need these created beings to resemble us so we can compare them to how great we claim to be? To establish superiority? Or are these just manifestations created to depict what we can't see inside ourselves?

In that case, yes, Genie. Monsters are <u>very</u> real. There <u>are</u> beings that want to suck everything from you and turn you into one of them. There <u>are</u> beings that do their best to hide in their woods or in their sea to be unknown. There <u>are</u> beings that roar with deep destructiveness, destroying everything that isn't as big as they are. We're all just created to wander from our labs, searching for someone to share days with while being afraid of getting burned in the process. Your fangs are on their way, Genie."

//

"So, Nikki loves the devil is what you're sayin'," said Morris, scarfing down the rest of his burger.

"No, no, no. It was her friend that started all

of it," I replied.

Morris looked a lot better than the last time I had seen him. He seemed to have somehow accepted what happened and was trying to figure it out. I told him not to say anything until we know what we were going to do. I hadn't really wrapped my head around it all, either. There was a substitute in our 1st hour class today, so we thought that would give us a little more time to talk. To our surprise, the teacher they brought in was a little more dedicated to watching students, so we decided we had to reconvene at lunch.

"Is there a way to track down the girl Nikki knew?" Morris asked.

"Nah, she said she hasn't seen her since that day. And none of the other people, either."

"Man, this is crazy."

"Yea, I know."

We finished our food and headed outside to the courtyard. There was an empty lunch table over by where the football players usually are. Their girlfriends must have been cold. We took it before someone came over to claim it.

"I wanted to ask Nikki more about what happened that day, but she was pretty upset," I said.

"That would be helpful," Morris replied.

"It was already hard for her to talk about. Plus, it was a while ago. I doubt she remembers. Kinda surprised she remembered as much as she did."

I push a cigarette butt through one of the holes of the table.

"Why did she let Raven from Teen Titans into y'all's house, though? Straight reckless," Morris asked.

"I just wanna know where that water came from. It saved my life," I said.

"Bruh, that was wild. I felt the energy all the way in the bathroom. And your clothes were completely dry," Morris' eyes widened as he remembered the scene he witnessed.

"Yours weren't."

"Yo, shut up."

A couple of quiet minutes passed. I was

usually good at putting pieces together. Like helping Morris get out of jams with girls or thinking of what to tell my mother to get Genie out of trouble. But that day? That day was something different. My mind couldn't conjure anything to make it all make sense. I took a moment to give my brain a break and watched the wind blow the snow around the courtyard. Something seemed familiar about the scene, and then I remembered. I had the weirdest dream Saturday night.

I was on an island. A beach or something. Standing on the edge of a grassy plateau. And the sky looked like it was going to storm soon. The gusts of wind were blowing extremely hard. Almost like a tornado. I remembered being cold, but I kept standing there trying to keep my balance from the gusts rushing past me. A million photographs were blowing in the wind from behind me into the sunset ahead. I could see somehow that they were pictures of my grandpa.

I slowly turned around and caught one of the photos. But it quickly turned to warm tears in my hand and fleeted through my fingers in the wind. Then I saw all the photographs shift at once, from looking away to staring straight at me. As they were passing, they began to shout out to me. They rushed past me, yelling "Return to the light! You're the one! Go back to the light!" His voice sounded so concerned for me. I remember losing my footing and falling backward off the plateau. Then, I woke up.

I told Morris the dream. He was as freaked out and confused as I was. Suddenly, he sprung up from his slouch with excitement.

"Bruh, we skippin' class!" he decided. I gave him the classic What-Are-You-Saying-Morris look he got from me every week.

"What do you mean?" I asked. He brought his face closer to mine with his eyes as big as he could make them.

"We are skipping class," he replied, in the best nerd impression he could pull off.

"Uh, why?" I asked.

"Because we gotta do some research on this mess!"

"How many classes are we skippin'? Where are we gonna go? I never skip class."

"You ain't never had a doctor turn into a boss battle and try to kill you, either. We're skippin' the rest of them. Come with me. I got a plan."

I got up and followed him toward the door to the inside of the school. I was a little nervous. I never had skipped class before. I wondered what would happen. I hoped his plan wasn't just sweet-talking the security guards into letting us just walk out. However, I could definitely say that he honestly seemed to know exactly what he was doing.

"I should trust him," I thought to myself. *"He seemed pretty sure that we weren't going to class."* And he had a point. We did need to figure out what had gone on. Something was after me. Maybe even my family. School could wait. I was curious about it myself. And if that doctor monster came back, I wanted to be ready. It wasn't too happy with me at the hospital.

We tucked into a darkened corner of the school near one of the side exits. Morris looked around to make sure the coast was clear while sliding his cell phone out of his pocket. He typed in his unlock code and started scrolling through his contacts. "Let's see, let's see," he whispered under his breath. The glow from his screen illuminated his face in the dim corner. He found who he was looking for, and I faintly hear the phone start to dial out.

"Keep a lookout," Morris mumbled quietly, not even making eye contact. His focus was impressive. Moving slowly to the edge of the wall, I looked both ways down the hall to see if anyone was coming. There was no sign of anyone. I looked back to give Morris my report, but he was looking down, waiting for whoever he was trying to reach to pick up. I rechecked the hallway, and there was still nothing there. "Ay, what's up?" Morris whispered into his phone from behind me. "I need one from you. Yea. I know, I got you," he said to the person on the phone.

I felt like the whole thing was a heist or something. I was officially blown away. I never realized Morris could be so organized. I decided then that I would never help him with homework again. While waiting for him to finish negotiating a price with his team, I heard something from the left by the exit. I carefully leaned over to find out what the noise was and see one of the school security guards walking towards us. I intensely walked back to Morris, who was still on the phone with his associate.

"Morris, we gotta go," I whispered, pulling on his coat sleeve.

"Hold up, this joker is tryin' to charge me double now!"

"No, Morris," I said more rigorously. "We gotta *go!*" I pointed over to where the guard was approaching from. Her footsteps were getting closer and closer. Morris pulled the phone away from his ear to listen. He finally heard the guard, and his eyes grew.

"The Suge's are coming!" he hissed to the person on the phone. The person tried to say something, but Morris interrupted. "Nevermind, I'll figure it out." He hung up the phone and pushed it back into his pocket.

Morris quickly looked around for an escape. The door to the library behind us was the only route we had time for. He pointed his head in the direction of the library, and we quickly headed that way. There were people studying there so we couldn't run through, or we were going to be busted for sure. But we had to get through the library and all the way to the door on the other side fast enough to not be seen by the guard.

The first shift of lunch kids were already in their classes while the second shift lunch should only be in the cafeteria or the courtyard. Also, there was a strict No Pass Policy around that time for kids like Morris who skipped class to go to both lunches. Morris had a lot of friends, but I always imagined he does it to get more food.

We pushed through the thick double doors and started power walking through the library. We slanted left to the passage along the edge. The library was sprinkled with people reading and studying. Ms. Cox, the school librarian, looked over her glasses at us to see who had just come in. I diverted my eyes to the doors in front of us on the other end before she recognized me. It was hard for me to keep up with Morris, but under the circumstances, I had to manage. He leaned over to me while taking a quick glimpse behind us.

"Listen. I'm gonna talk to you, and you just pretend to be listening super deep. OK?" Morris asked. I tried to respond, but I was getting more and more out of breath the further we went. I didn't realize the library was as big as it was until I had to rush through it. "We're going to jail," I said between heavy breaths. "They're gonna tase us and tackle us and arrest us and put us in juvi for skippin' class. Do you know who else skipped class? Criminals probably!" I noticed the air open up behind us as the guard made her way into the library. My heart picked up speed as I heard her heavy boots marching towards us.

"Yea, yea, yea. So, politics and stuff. Sports and hot dogs. Or whatever," Morris ranted, nervously. I could tell he hadn't done this part before. I hastefully nodded my head.

"Oh, yea. Politics. It's crazy," I said just as nervously. I guess I hadn't done this before, either.

"Yea, me too. I don't even know how he did that."

"That was wild. The part where he did it."

I tried to focus on the nonsense, but I knew the guard was right behind us. It was hard not to look back. But if I did, we were done for. I started to say something else dumb to Morris, but I heard the guard call out to us. "Hey, you two." I could tell she was trying to lower her voice for the students that were in the library. My heart was still about to blast out of my chest. We kept racing toward the door ahead.

"Because to *me*… to *me*, mermaids are monsters because I can't swim," Morris tremored. I saw a few of the kids look over at us out of the corner of my eye. One of them tried to wave at us to get our attention, thinking we didn't know the guard was talking to us, but I pretended I didn't notice.

"Yea, like a refrigerator? When was it fridged the *first* time? What's going on here?" I asked back. It felt like the way out moving further and further away from us.

"Hey!" the guard said more intensely. She seemed less worried about being discreet now. Her footsteps were on beat with the pounding in my chest. My mouth was starting to get dry. Morris was doing all the talking at that point. I had condensed all my responses to "yea's" and "uh huh's". I could almost imagine her hand on my shoulder.

Then out of nowhere, a bunch of rapid muffled popping sounds above us disrupted the library's quiet hum. I briefly froze from the shock of the noise that filled the atmosphere, but Morris tugged my arm. I followed his hint and kept racing towards the way out of the infinite room. "The Firecracker Kid!" someone shouted.

The sound of chairs dragging on the floor as kids stood up multiplied with every second. The guard started running the other direction away from us, toward the firecrackers upstairs. "Stay seated!" said the security guard as she burst back through the doors behind us. We use the distraction to run the rest of the way out of the library and then out the other side exit of the school.

"How do you go through this every day? Just go to class!" I panted.

"*Refrigerators*? You literally asked me about *refrigerators*?" replied Morris.

"You know I don't know anything about mermaids!"

He took his phone back out of his pocket and ordered a ride to his house. I leaned against the blind side of the building to catch my breath. "I think we should be good now," Morris said, typing something on his phone. "No one really comes to the side exits until later." After a few moments of waiting, Morris' phone buzzes. "They're pulling up," he said, scanning the nearby parking lot for the car. I walked with him to the parking lot and saw the dark blue sedan come to meet us.

"Yo, shoutout that Firecracker Kid everyone is always talkin' about. That was perfect timing. They've been looking for them all year. I wonder if they caught him," I said as I opened the door to the car.

"Yea. But I'm still not paying him double," Morris replied.

"Wow, Morris."

I shook my head as I got into the vehicle.

CHAPTER 10

"Fear is darkness. It isn't there. It can't be touched. It can't speak. It has no essence. But it is so controlling. Demanding. It's so obsessed with us. It wants to <u>be</u>. It wants to take. So bad. It makes sense that people become 'possessed' in movies. Darkness wants to be noticed. It also makes sense why people are so afraid of darkness conquering. I can genuinely say the idea of being paralyzed by fear is honest. The biggest objective of any dark 'being' is to make you scared. An attempt to frighten is a test of intelligence. If it can scare you into thinking the invisible unknown is

stronger, it is."

//

Morris' house was amazing. Everything looked brand new. Like in magazines. The whole house had a white, black, and gray theme. Gray sofas with white pillows. White coffee table with a weird black vase and flowers. Black kitchen cabinets with gray handles. They had the first refrigerator with a screen built into it that I had ever seen. It was definitely how I wanted my house to look when I got older.

Morris ran upstairs to get his laptop. I waited for him in the kitchen. The stools for the kitchen island were so soft. It felt better than I thought it would to sit and relax. It was so weird being in another house. The smell was different. The air that filled the spaces around me felt so peaceful. I couldn't think of the proper words to describe it. It felt like I was in a whole new world.

It nearly brought me to tears thinking of how I

could have potentially been living. I looked toward the living room and noticed a few pictures of Morris' family. Everyone was smiling. Real smiles. Morris would tell me about his twin sisters, but I'd never seen them before. They looked exactly like him. The whole place felt so put together. I couldn't help but think I polluted it. Like I didn't belong there. I started to get up to wait outside until I heard Morris coming back downstairs.

"OK. Let's do this," he said, opening up his large silver laptop.

"What do we look up?" I asked.

"I don't know. I thought you knew," he laughed. "Let's try... 'Sister lets people come over that tries to kill everybody in the house during the summer'". To his surprise, no results came up.

We brainstormed for a second, and then I blurted out the first thing that made sense to me. "Do 'fruit spell' or something like that," I suggested. Morris typed that into the search engine, and a list of websites filled the computer screen. Blogs, forums, and tutorials on people talking about had been called the "Mijenta fruit spell".

There were a lot of different-looking people in the video thumbnails. A lot of tattoos. Some with piercings all over their faces. A few had crazy makeup on. But there were also some normal-looking people. People you wouldn't think would know anything about spells. Some of the video titles were about Midland and its misinformed citizens claiming to obtain magic. One of the thumbnails looked like the person had been crying. I noticed Morris look over at me.

"So, what do we go to?" asked Morris.

"I guess the first one," I replied.

Morris moved the cursor to the first website. It looked like an online forum. He clicked the link, and there was a question at the top of the page in addition to a few hundred comments. The question asked if the spell was real or just made up for fun. We scrolled through the answers, and it looked like a bunch of people speculating. A few seemed pretty sure. A couple of the comments said it involved the Midland government. Others said kids were just messing around. But what I saw in the hospital was far from "messing around."

After scrolling through a few pages of sketchy search results, we found a thumbnail of a bald woman who looked intensely at us through the screen. The video was titled "Slain member of The Facinelli Family warns NOT Do The Mijenta Fruit Spell". The video seemed to be re-uploaded from another channel. "That one," I said, pointing at the woman staring back at us. Morris started the video. It began with soundless white text on a dark background. The words read:

"The following video is about the Mijenta Fruit Spell. Watch at your own risk. I am not responsible for what happens to you if you have already completed the spell. Only watch this video during the day."

Just the warning gave me chills all over my body. "Holy bleep!" Morris yelled out loud. We both seemed to have come to a silent agreement: this video was the real deal.

"Hello," the woman said in her hushed tone. "I can't tell you my name, but it is important to know that I am a member of The Facinelli Family. This video is real, and I can assure you this isn't any kind of joke." Her eyes didn't waver from the camera. It was like she was talking right to us. Her thin figure sat still in the frame of the video. The dark clothing blending in with the dim background of the video made her look somewhat like a floating head. I was completely entranced by her seriousness.

"If you are watching this, you are probably aware of why," the woman said. "I will briefly explain the spell. Please know that this video isn't for fun or any kind of tutorial. I will share my personal knowledge and the consequences of interacting with these elements. I will not be answering any questions." Morris paused the video.

"Bruh..." he said, looking downward. "She ain't playin'."

"Yea, this is crazy," I replied.

"You sure you wanna do this?"

"I don't think I have a choice."

I wiped my sweaty hands on my pant leg and unpaused the video before I decided to change my mind. "The fruit, known as "The Mijenta fruit", has come from a time before time itself," the woman said. "No one knows exactly where the tree it grows on came from. The original fruit was soft and round. Blue and purplish in color. The diluted version seen today does not compare in its beauty. The initial use was something different than the spell most know of. It has since been altered. Now, with the appropriate words spoken from the book it is often accompanied with, it is to maliciously link your thoughts, ideas, self-control, and feelings to the fruit for the taking."

"A people in a time before us, a loving people of peace and nobility, used the fruit for a sacred ritual. A ritual to pass their knowledge from one generation to the next. This was to ensure the stories and lessons from ancestors were not lost as time went on. It preserved the rich history of the people. Only one chosen person in a generation was given the responsibility of carrying on the legacy of the prior generations. The person was referred to as The Elder."

"Once a new Elder was chosen by the previous Elder, they would partake in the ritual to obtain their new selves. The new Elder would eat the fruit from a sacred tree, and this would fill them with the wisdom that had been granted to the people for centuries. Then, the knowledge of the people would transfer from the previous Elder to the new one."

"However, a terrible event took place in Midland centuries ago where the ritual and the knowledge of the people were stolen from them through manipulation and greed. The people had stolen what belonged to them by my family, The Facinelli Family, who has sought after the souls of many others ever since. The ritual, meant to be of beauty and immense reverence of history, has been perverted into a devious trick that we know today as the Mijenta Fruit Spell."

"The spell has been spread to many places, but began when my family settled in Midland long ago. It is now used to capture the very souls of those who partake in the spell. The person's thought, ability to control themselves consistently and use of feelings belong to my family and the darkness we are in agreement with."

"Please know that even though this ritual was initially used for good, the spell or anything of the sort is now meant to harm you. The benefits some say they feel are eventually destructive. There is absolutely nothing good about the spell. If you have partaken in the spell, please understand that things may be too late for you. But if you are lucky enough to have a chance, you must locate one of the components from the *original* ritual."

"The book. The original book, the real one, is necessary if you are to make anything better for yourself after this. Not one of the altered copies you may have purchased. The original is the key."

"Great," I said.

"If we don't know who has the original book, or where they are, how are we supposed to do anything?" Morris replied, finishing my thought.

The worry and hopelessness wrapped

themselves around me. I tried to release myself from it but there wasn't anything I could do to help me. In the meantime, I shook my head in cluelessness and returned my attention to the video.

"Once you open the book, be very cautious. Certain phrases should not be repeated. Some can't be undone once spoken..." The woman stopped and looked up for a moment. Her dimmed room and low video quality made it hard to see her face clearly. But she seemed to be blinking away tears from her eyes. She continued with the same tamed urgency as before.

"Search for the page that has images resembling burning fruit and split bodies. You will have to repeat the words on that page in the clearest manner you can manage. There will be a bitter, metal-like taste in your mouth as you speak the words. Heaviness of the tongue will occur. An urge to swallow will soon follow. This is said Mijenta fruit's true taste."

I pictured the taste in my mind as being like pennies. Or like a mouth full of batteries. I wondered how the woman could be wrong if she knew all the information so thoroughly. She seemed so sure. It was hard to question what she was saying. I glanced at Morris who still had his attention locked into the video. I decided to focus again on what she was saying too.

"Soon a presence will be felt around you," the woman said. She paused for a second and needed a deep breath to continue. "Its shadow will consume your light. The darkness will blend with who you are. Who you believe yourself to be. It will need to be a part of you for you to remove what you've done to yourself."

The woman's words held me in place. The gravity of time was the most evident at that moment. As she continued, the seriousness forced my heart to run harder. The blood within me heated. I realized that there may not be much of an escape from what happened to me. But I had to try. If I wanted to live.

"Everything you think you gained or have been granted from the spell will be taken from you. Once within you, the presence will take what belongs to it. Moments after, the figure will come out and vanish from the room."

Morris paused the video.

"Yo! That's kind of what you said Nikki told you!" Morris shouted.

"Yea, it's kinda similar. But this is different. What happened to me wasn't the same as most people who do this," I replied.

"That's true."

Morris took a moment to think over the details.

"One thing I remember Nikki said sticks out about this part," I said. "She said the presence was mad."

"I bet he was mad 'cuz you messed up the normal way of doing the spell! That's the only thing that makes sense!" exclaimed Morris.

"I think I'm the only one that's actually *bitten* the fruit. That explains why they were looking for me."

"Yea! Nikki said the person that showed up was going to find who messed up the process of the spell! He thought it was one of them! But it was you!"

I thought back to what Nikki told me happened that day. Morris was right. The presence would be looking for which one of Nikki's friends would have symptoms of the true ritual the whole time, not the spell, but none of them had it. When it saw me, it probably thought I was just a baby and had nothing to do with it."

"I thought back at all the times where people would tell me I was smarter than I should be at my age. Wiser. Like I had lived lives before me. I finally understood why. And it also explained the dream I had with the people running. But I still had no clue what was happening to them. I tapped the space bar on his laptop to continue the video.

"There will be a series of events that take place after you reverse the spell. If you can. An increase in hunger, severe emotional shifts instead of numbness, disrupted focus and many other things could occur. The exact opposite of what took place when you did the spell. This could vary depending on a number of things." The woman seemed to be hurt. Something was bothering her about having to talk about what she knew. We could tell this was difficult for her to explain. But her perseverance was encouraging.

Her voice began to waver. She seemed to be wanting to speak her next words carefully. After a brief moment, the surety returned to her posture. "There is something very important for you to know. There is a time limit you have to complete this. You will have until what's called "The Hour of Completion" on "The Day of Understanding" to undo any effects of the Mijenta spell. That translates to 7:00 pm, or sundown, on the day you gained the knowledge I'm giving you in this video. This was originally left for any new Elders to reject their new life and return to what they knew before."

A deep breath escaped from his lungs. But then I realized the time was creeping up fast. I had less than half of the day left. Flashes of the dream of my grandpa from the other night echoed in my mind. *"Return to the light! You're the one! Go back to the light!"* I recalled Dr. Coleman transforming at the hospital. His evil eyes. I stared at the video again to rid my mind of his stare.

"I need you to listen to me, and you need to listen *closely*. You need to find the book. Do whatever you can to find it. I wish I could help you further, but only a few members of the family have been shown where it is. I have not been allowed to see it. The book will be hard to retrieve. But if you want your life back, you have no choice. This is the most important piece of information you will ever receive. You must get the book. It is in a hidden location. You don't have time to waste. You have to go *now*."

"If you are watching this and have any time left, you need to turn this off *right now* and find the book." Tears began to rapidly stream down her face. Her lips started to quiver more and more. There was no effort from her to wipe her face or to disrupt her gaze from the viewer. She was staring right into me. Begging my soul to take heed. "You *have* to find it." The video ended.

"It's about 1:30, Morris," I said softly. We were both frozen stiff. He didn't respond. "We have around 5 hours to find the book. And it can be anywhere." Silence remained with us longer than welcomed. My mind started churning. "There's got to be a way around this." I looked back at the screen, then at Morris, and then to the floor. "Think, Braxton," I murmured to myself.

"What do we do?" Morris asked.

"We have to find Nikki. She's the only one we know that knows anything about where we can start looking. She's the only one that can help us," I replied.

Morris closed his laptop and stood up from his stool. "Let's go."

CHAPTER 11

"*I wonder if butterflies remember being caterpillars.*

No one evolves so dramatically. So elegantly.

Caterpillars spend their lives crawling, barely able to

look up at the world above them. Labeled as simply a

bug. Barely even being noticed or talked about. Then,

eventually going away, falling deeper into solitude.

Further into what is unseen by most. Only to emerge

with wings that take them to the sky hidden from

them.

Once they change, who teaches them to fly? Was the

thought of flight always within them? Do they go

THEN, A BOY

back and take notice of the caterpillar soon to be in the air with them, or forget them as they were forgotten before?

//

The parking lot of Nikki's job was calm and gentle. There was barely anyone else there. That made things a little easier. We stepped out of the rideshare, and the vehicle hummed off into the winter afternoon. I led the way into the front entrance of the hotel. The warm air met us as the automatic doors parted ways for us to enter. It smelled clean inside. The waterfall fountain ran steadily down a bunch of pre-established rocks. Big-screen TVs were on either side of the front desk rotated slides of room photos and attractions in the area.

I looked around, but there was no sign of Nikki anywhere. She told me she worked all over the building. It was fairly large, so I didn't want to wander around to find her. Plus, I was sure the adults working there were wondering why we weren't in school on a Monday afternoon.

We risked heading to the two people at the front desk. There was a thin blonde-haired woman and a tall olive-skinned guy with glasses. They both looked like robots in their hotel uniforms. They were oddly generic-looking, prepped in a way that would seem like a picture in a magazine. Both were smiling for nothing and seemingly very happy to be at work that day. The guy was on a phone call, so we spoke to the robot lady.

"Hello! How can I help you today?" She said pleasantly.

"I'm looking for Nikki. Is she here?" I asked.

"Oh, you must be her brother, Braxton!"

"Yea, that's me."

"Wow! It's nice to finally meet you! She's told me so much about you! Hold on just a second."

She bent down for a quick second and came back up with her cell phone. "I'll send her a text to let her know you're here." She proceeded to tap around on the screen. I leaned against the desk and watched a few of the slides cycle through on the televisions.

"Aren't you two supposed to be in school?" The android lady asked.

"There was an infestation at our school. Butterpillars." Morris lied. I looked down so she didn't see me rolling my eyes. The woman's gasp was more shocking than Morris' ability to keep a straight face. "Yea," he continued. "The cocoons froze and cracked open. The caterpillars weren't done changing yet so the monstrosities were flying around the school trying to understand themselves. It was pretty traumatizing. So, the principal sent us home."

"Oh no! I know that must have been terrible! Are you guys OK?" the lady asked in utter shock.

"Yea, but it's really hard to talk about." Morris put a hand over his eyes to cover his fake tears. "I was really trying to study and learn stuff in class. We're here to talk to Nikki for some advice on how to handle this." I leaned over and patted him on the back for "support", wondering if I would ever go through metamorphosis and change into what Morris was one of these days.

The robot lady was devastated. She quickly

picked her phone from the desk to call Nikki. Before she could dial out, Nikki came through one of the doors from behind the front desk.

"Hicks! Morris? What are you guys doing here? Morris, why are you crying?" she asked.

"We need to talk," I replied.

She motioned us back towards the door she came from.

"Could you cover for me, Janet?" Nikki asked the robot lady.

"Take all the time you need," she replied, concerningly.

We came around the desk and went through the royal blue door. The short hallway led to an elevator. Morris immediately dropped the crying act. Nikki saw him and glared at me.

"Ay! I didn't tell him to do all that!" I defended.

She tucked her tongue into her jaw.

"If you two are here playin' around, I -" she blurted.

"No." I interrupted. "We're not playin'. This is

for real."

She sensed the seriousness in my tone and knew something was wrong. The elevator took us down into an employee break area. Nikki scanned her employee card and opened the door for us.

A line of different vending machines along the blue walls. There were a couple of pool tables to the right of the entrance on top of grassy green carpets. The neon pool sticks mounted under the large television slowly pulsed through a series of bright colors. The news channel's chatter was noticeable but not distracting. Light clanks from the ice machine on the far end of the room gently echoed against the big silver refrigerator next to it. A pinball machine and a few old arcade games I didn't recognize the names of caught Morris' attention. We followed Nikki to one of the round white tables close to the middle of the room. She grabbed a nearby chair and sat with us.

"So, what's going on?" She asked.

I looked at Morris to see which one of us was going to start. He looked back but didn't say anything, so I jumped into it.

"It's about that day you told me about. The day with the book and the fruit," I replied.

Nikki's head dropped as she breathed deeply recalling the incident. She glanced over her shoulder to make sure no one else was in the break room.

"Hicks..." she started.

"I looked into it today. *We* looked into it. And we need your help," I pleaded.

She looked at me, concerned.

"You didn't do it, did you?" she asked.

"No, no, no. We didn't do it. But we watched a video of someone who knew about it."

"It's probably fake," Nikki said. "People post dumb videos about that spell all the time.

"The video we found was for real. It was a woman from an old family that had something to do with it. I found out I messed it up. It wasn't supposed to go how it did," I said.

Nikki scooted closer to the table. A confused look covered her face. It was then that I realized she probably had tried to forget that whole thing ever happened. So, I started from the beginning. I explained what we learned from the video. The intended process. How our incident was different. The effects. And the search for the original book. She entered into the cloud of fear that had been over us for the past hour.

"So, we need to know where the original book is. Fast," I said in conclusion.

"If there's any other kind of book, I've never seen it, Hicks," replied Nikki.

"It's not the same book. The version that everyone's been using is just a copy. The original one has other stuff in it that we need. We just-"

"Hicks." She dropped her look to finish realizing what her words meant, then lifted her gaze back to me. Her eyes began to well up with tears. "I have no clue where that book is."

The busy hum of the room seemed to rise in my ears. My mouth began to dry up. All the oxygen fled from the room. All that was left, all that existence consisted of at that moment, were her words. "Braxton!" Morris shouted, snapping his fingers repeatedly. I staggered back into reality. My eyes unfogged and refocused on him and Nikki. "Sorry," I said softly under my breath. I sat still wondering what the next hours could mean for me.

"There's got to be *something*!" Morris shouted desperately. "Where is the shop she went to? Who were those other people she had with her? Where are they at?"

"I don't know where she got it. Like I said, I couldn't go with her. And I haven't seen those people since then. I didn't even know the other ones, really. Just Melody. I heard she moved. She didn't say bye. I heard overheard someone say she left," Nikki replied.

Silence interrupted once again. I turned my attention to the television behind Nikki's head. The weatherman was trying to keep his balance in the storm he was trapped in. Dirty, gray wet snow was like a filter over the screen. Debris flung in and out of the frame. One of the weatherman's hands held his microphone, while the other was on his head, keeping his hat pinned down.

Cars crept behind him. The gusts were harsh. The weatherman lifted his hand to push up his thick glasses and his hat quickly flew off of his head. He whipped around to catch it but quickly saw that it was long gone. Then he turned back around to the camera. But it was not the weatherman anymore. It was my grandpa. He looked just like he did in the pictures from the dream I had. I squinted to make sure what I was seeing was real. It definitely was.

He slowly walked closer to the camera, looking more and more afraid with each step. Once close enough, he leaned into the camera until all I could see was his face. It felt like there was no such thing as anything else. Just me and the television. Then I saw him mouth the words to me that he had told me before in my dream: "Return to the light.". I sprung up out of my chair, quickly running back into actuality.

"LOOK!" I screamed, pointing at the television. Nikki and Morris very quickly turned towards it. But just milliseconds before, a "Please Stand By" message covered the screen. They looked back at me, confused while I stood there panting. It was gone.

"What is your problem?" Nikki asked.

"It was grandpa! It was really him!" I replied.

Nikki's confusion transformed to pity. "No, I'm serious!" I pleaded. Her expression stayed the same. "He keeps telling me to return to a light. I don't know what that means. But it must be something," I said. I sat back down, finally ready to be a part of the solution. Morris was still dazed by my outburst. I put all the pieces of information together and decided to start from the beginning. I went back to the story Nikki told me before.

"What kind of place did your friend get the book from?" I asked.

"I don't remember her saying the name. She only mentioned it was some kind of store or shop," replied Nikki.

"What about where it was? Do you have any idea?"

"I never asked."

"OK... Did she have a car? Did her parents let her use theirs?"

"No, I don't think she had her *own* car. But

one of her boyfriends would sometimes let her drive his. I think it was just to skip classes and stuff. She said they would usually go to his house."

"Would you have any idea where he lived?"

"I think it was over by the mall. On the east side."

"OK. Morris, let me see your phone."

Morris scrambled around his pocket until he got ahold of his cell phone. He quickly unlocked it and slid it across the table. I grabbed it and opened the internet app. I searched for a list of malls we had in Midland. Then I scrolled through the small list, searching for anything on that side of the city. The Bluegills Mall was the only match. I clicked on their website.

There were pictures of the local team it was named after and a bunch of pictures of the different stores it had inside. After scrolling for a second, I found links for the list of the mall's stores. I looked for *any* place that looked like it would sell books. Nothing seemed to be a good enough result. I double-checked the list to see if there was anything remotely close that I could have missed but couldn't see anything useful.

"What are you thinkin'?" Nikki asked, curiously.

"I want to see if there are any bookstores or anything like that in the mall that she could have gone to," I replied.

"Good call. How about around the mall?" Morris suggested.

"Yea, check around that area!" Nikki agreed. "That's a great idea."

They both shifted their chairs next to mine to get a better view of the phone. I copied the address of the mall from the bottom of their website. Closing the internet window, I scrolled through the app list until I spotted the Map application. I tapped it and pasted the address into the search bar.

The location of the mall zoomed in, displaying information for the mall and ratings from previous customers. I zoomed out to check the surrounding area. There were a bunch of random businesses I hadn't heard of before. I had never been to that side of town. My mom would have never brought us there. I drug the map up and down to find something even remotely close to a place that would have the kind of book someone would buy for the spell. We were all staring down, antagonizing the phone for results, when Nikki grabbed my arm.

"Wait," she said, honing in on the screen. "Let me see this."

I handed her the phone. Morris and I leaned over to try to spot what she was looking at.

"What is it?" I asked.

"Hold on," she replied.

She tapped the phone a couple of times and zoomed in on something. It seemed to confirm whatever she was thinking. "I think this is it," Nikki said.

I grabbed the phone from her. Confused, I sucked my teeth. Morris snatched the phone from me to see what the problem was. He pulled his head back and scrunched his face. "That logo," she explained. "That logo looks kinda like the one I saw on the bag she brought over." I leaned back over to the phone to take another look.

The logo was a tonearm of a turntable standing up vertically with two triangles pointing out of the left and right of the end of it. It was all encircled with a record in the background. Nikki continued to plead her case. We looked it over for a second and zoomed back out from the picture to see where the place was. Then I saw the name.

"Wow… Wait," I said, putting my hand over my mouth.

"What, what, what?" Morris asked frantically.

"That's got to be it. We're going there."

"But it's not a bookstore! Or a weird shop!"

"It's at least worth a shot. What else are we gonna do?"

"Getting way over there and finding out it's a waste of time is *not* worth a shot, Braxton."

"You have any better ideas?" I asked.

Morris sat still for a few seconds and threw his hands up in the air "I guess not," he said

I got up from the table, and Morris stood up after me.

"Wait, what are you guys gonna do?" Nikki said, rising from her seat with us.

"We're gonna see if this is the place. We have to at least try," I replied. I felt like I sounded a lot braver than I was.

"How do you know it's there? I mean, the logo looks familiar, but I don't know what that means. Maybe I'm trippin'. It was so long ago."

"Nikki, we're goin'." I decided to keep the brave demeanor on for a little while longer to help me get out the door without throwing up or crying. I leaned over to hug her, but she tilted away to look at me.

"Hicks... I can't let you do this. I know I said I would help you bu-"

"But what, Nikki?" I asked, a little more sternly than I meant to sound. "What do you want me to do? Go home and clean the house until somethin' knocks on the door to kill me? I gotta try *somethin'*."

Nikki stared at me for a while, not knowing what to say. Tears started to slowly make their way down her cheeks. She looked at me as if she realized something. Like something new just happened inside her. She lunged towards me and gave me the biggest hug I think I'd ever gotten in my life.

"I love you, Hicks," she wept. Her tears leaked into my hair and down my scalp, giving me chills.

"Love you too."

We eventually peeled apart. She took another moment to look at me. Her eyes seemed like scales had fallen off and she was seeing something new for the first time. She gave Morris a quick touch on the shoulder. I noticed that he was holding back tears too, but there was no need to bring it up.

We all seemed to inwardly sigh at the same time and headed back toward the elevator. On the way back up, Morris tapped in another order for a ride on his phone. I took a glance at the robot lady, who waved to us on the way out of the lobby door. I smiled back and stood outside in the winter air with Morris. We didn't say anything until just before the car pulled up for us.

"You ready for all this?" Morris asked.

"Nah. Probably not," I replied.

We stepped inside the car and headed towards our new destination.

The Lighthouse Records Store.

CHAPTER 12

"I've never been a fan of rushing. I never understood the need for it. The act of arriving at your destination before the person you are mistreating arrives at theirs is not rewarded. The people already at the place you are racing to won't even ask what things you did to get there.

I used to wonder why my mom would race past someone on the road, just to almost catapult us out of the car when she smashed the brake pedal.

We always ended up at the same red light as them and she would try not to look over at them. It's weird how people turn into vehicles in our minds when they're not walking. Your entire being transforms from a thinking living breathing soul into a two-ton piece of meaningless metal the second you step foot in a vehicle. Accidents aren't accidents. They're results."

//

Our driver would not shut up. Morris was pretty decent at talking to people, in my opinion, and even he was running out of small talk. That is when I remembered I left my mp3 player and Big House Edition headphones at the hospital. I would have almost risked another run-in with that doctor monster to go get them if it meant I didn't have to listen to the driver talk anymore. *"Why do some people feel like if they stop talking, the world is missing out?"*, I thought. He eased into a red light and took the opportunity to turn around and look directly into our faces.

"You guys like you could use a nap!" he

laughed. "Boy, I know what you mean. This is a good day for a nice big ole' nap!"

"Yea," Morris acknowledged, looking out the window.

"There was a time when I was driving early in the morning. I was *completely* worn out, I tell you. I thought, you know, if I don't take a little nap, I could be in some real big trouble."

I saw the traffic light change green behind his head through the window.

"The light's green," I murmured.

"*What's* that? The guy replied, directing his look just at me.

I pointed at the green light in front of us. The driver turned back around. "Oh!" he said, pulling through the intersection. I gazed out the window and watched the snowy wind blow past us. Drops of melted snow streaked into one another until they were out of my sight. Snowplows scrapped against the street as they bullied the snow onto the timid sidewalks.

"Hey, have you two heard this guy before?"

The driver blurted, looking at me through the rearview mirror. He turned up the radio that I didn't notice before. An angry voice got louder and louder as he moved the dial. "Ain't this a bunch of bologna?" the driver shouted over the voice. "How the heck are you gonna keep jacking up the taxes of the working man and expect us to take care of our families?"

The car slowed to another stop at a red light. The driver guy gripped the shoulder of the passenger seat and turned around to me again. "*I* say, you sell one of those mansions of yours you got instead of digging in my pockets every day!"

I nodded as if I wasn't fifteen years old. I looked over at Morris, who managed to fall asleep really *really* fast. I didn't appreciate him leaving me to deal with this driver by myself. *"I'm fighting him later,"* I thought to myself. The driver noticed me look over at Morris. He faced back forward and glanced at him in his rearview mirror. "See? He's got the right idea!" he laughed. Morris cracked one eye open and looked at me with a grin. Smart. I wished I had thought of that first. *"Oh, yea. I'm definitely fighting him later."*

Someone behind us honked their horn, and our driver quickly sped ahead. "Sorry!" he shouted, waving his hand in the air. The record store was on the completely other side of the city. I couldn't see where we were or how much longer we had left. Morris had the info on his phone in his pocket. Plus, I couldn't make out the distance from the driver's GPS. It felt like we'd been in the car forever. I tried to find something else to focus on. But I couldn't. I looked back out the window for any clues of our whereabouts.

We seemed to be going a less busy route. Some kind of back road. I wasn't sure. I began to calculate if we had enough time to handle this or if the book could really be at the record store. It was hard not to let doubt creep in. I didn't know of any record stores that sold books, but it was my only chance. I had no other plans. I started to try to put the time together in my head.

"We left school close to the end of the 2nd

lunch period, which was around 1:00, got the ride to Morris' house and was there for a little over an hour. That was around 2:30. Then, we left there and got to Nikki's job, maybe within 20 minutes or so. I don't know how long we were talking, but it couldn't have been more than an hour. That means it was probably somewhere around 4:30 pm or so."

"I don't think I'll be able to be home in time to not get in trouble, but at least I'll be alive. I'm so glad we found out this so soon. I really gotta thank Morris for dragging me into skipping school. Even though it'll cost me another day in the Big House. It's better than costing me my life. I guess."

I could overhear the driver arguing with the angry man on the radio. I couldn't wait to get out of the car. "Well, it's your fault he's in office in the first place! People like you are the reason we have to work so hard!" he shouted. I could tell he was getting more and more worked up. But I didn't care what he did. As long as he kept talking to himself and not me.

It was really hard to ignore him, though. I discovered at that point that Morris started actually trying to sleep. I looked forward and noticed the driver looking at me again through his rearview mirror. "This guy's such a damn jackass! There's no way he honestly thinks we are going to consolidate households just so we can get by!" He hollered. His loud voice shook Morris up. "Yea," the driver said, "I agree that population is getting up there in numbers, but we can't just-"

Suddenly the sound of brakes squealing next to us ended the conversation. The dirty silver pickup truck screeched towards us from the left side of the road. Before there was any time to react, the vehicle blasted into us at what felt like a million miles per hour. Everything went black.

I woke up with someone pulling my arm. Everything was blurred, and my head and neck were killing me. There were a lot of people talking. Lights flashed all around me. I could faintly smell the scent of gasoline. I tried to say something, but I couldn't seem to manage to get anything out. I was freezing cold. I felt my legs being dragged through the winter snow.

Sounds went in and out from being muffled to being too loud every few seconds. Slight heat streaked down the right side of my face. I slowly lifted my shaky hand to graze my cheek. The dark warm blood quickly became cold over my knuckles. I repeatedly blinked to help my eyes focus. After a few moments, I gradually remembered what happened.

A few people surrounded the car we were all in. I tried to peak through the tiny crowd to see if there was any sign of Morris. After a couple of moments, I saw them drag him out of the back of the car. He looked limp for a second. I started to worry, but not for long. I picked up on him looking around to see what's going on through the legs of the people around us.

I looked past the front of the upside-down car and saw an ambulance with someone being pushed into the back of it. The frame of the person looked like our driver. It looked like he got the brunt of the impact. I briefly felt bad for being so annoyed by him. But I had to make sure Morris is OK.

I noticed the sky was slightly darker than

before. More details of what was going on slowly crept back into my mind. *"How long have we been out?"* I thought. I instantly started to panic. I gathered my strength and tried to get up but ended up tipping over in the heap of snow next to me.

Someone touched my shoulder. "Woah, woah, woah," they said. "Slow down, tiger." I didn't know what Spider-Man comic they had been reading, but I didn't have time for 'woah, woah, woah'. I tried to get up again, but this time, I felt the hand press me back down. "How about you rest for a minute? We'll have someone over here shortly to help you and your friend."

I looked up to see who was pissing me off. It was a tall police officer, over 6 feet maybe. He was clean-shaven with a hat that darkened his eyes. I looked through the fence of legs to my right and saw a paramedic flashing a light into Morris' eyes. We seemed to share the same mindset. He was avoiding the light and trying to get up.

"Move! I'm fine," I heard him shout. "Hey!" The officer next to me yelled while walking over to

Morris. I took the opportunity to try to get up again. I took a deep breath and readied my legs for the effort. I slowly lifted myself up onto one knee and waited to still myself. Then I rose onto my other leg. I paused for a second before getting too ahead of myself. When my legs started to wake up, I experimented with taking a step. I put one foot in front of me and pulled forward. Then, I tried it again. It seemed to be working. It seemed like I had been lying there for a while. The officer saw me and wasn't happy.

"What do you think you're doing?" he asked sternly. "I thought I told you to be still!"

"I'm fine. I just need to check on my friend," I replied.

"Your friend is fine! You need to have a seat!"

"If he's fine, why are you still here?"

"We need to have you two file a report! The driver is being rushed to the hospital, and the other driver is unconscious! You two are the only available witnesses of the accident!"

I looked back to where I saw the ambulance in front of the car. It was gone. I peered over at

Morris, who seemed to have decided to comply with the medics to make sure he was OK.

"What time is it?" I asked the officer.

"It's a quarter after 5." He replied.

"It's a quarter after 5?" I thought. *"As in 5:15? We've got to get out of here. Fast."* I searched my mind for a lie to use. "I need to call my mom," I lied. The officer hesitated but eventually shuffled around for his phone in his pocket. He surfaced a small gray device and swiped the wet screen off with his pant leg.

"Make it quick," he demanded, extending the phone to me. I started to take it, but then my inner Morris kicked in. "I don't have the number memorized. I have to use my brother's phone." I scared myself at how quickly I came up with the lie. The officer looked over at Morris and then back at me. Upset to have to humble himself, he let me walk over to Morris.

"Ay. You good?" Morris asked when I got to him.

"Yea, I'll live. Maybe. It's after 5. We gotta

go," I replied.

"Dang, for real?" He strained his hurt arm to her his hand into his pocket for his phone. "Oh bleep. What took them so long to get to us?"

"I'm sure it was the weather. There have accidents all day, probably."

"Makes sense. We were on back roads too."

"That cop said we gotta stay here and file reports or whatever."

"Nah, forget all that," Morris replied, looking around through the wreckage for a way out.

"Yea, that's what I said. I told him I needed to use your phone to call our mom. But I'm sure he's gonna be bothering us soon. How far away from the record store are we?"

Morris checked his phone again and checked his GPS app for the location.

"We're about 20 minutes away. Probably 30 with the snow," he said.

A heavy breath shot out from me. I started to look around for an escape when Morris interrupted my thought.

"We got to figure something out," I said.

"Like what?" asked Morris.

"I don't know, but let's get away from here for now," I replied.

I looked over at the cop who was examining the debris from the crash. The medics were with the driver that hit us, who seemed to be in and out of consciousness. A few cars were creeping through the street, trying to get a good look at what happened. One of the vehicles brought to my attention a gas station on the corner of the street. "There!" I whispered to Morris, pointing in the direction of the building. He followed close behind, careful not to groan too much from the pain.

I wasn't sure if we would have another chance, so we had to be as quiet as possible. We slowly backed up, step by step, attempting to ease our way out of the potential view of the officer. We inched away more and more until we felt it was safe enough to turn our backs to the scene. We picked up speed and raced towards the building. We took a few instances to look back and make sure we were still in the clear. We were about ten steps away from the door when we heard the officer yell out for us.

"Hey! Where did those two boys go?" he shouted to someone at the car wreck. I couldn't make out any answering him. We jolted to the gas station as fast we could manage. I twinge my eyes shut at the soreness in my body. Just when I thought it was a wrap for us, we made it to the front of the store. I noticed our tracks in the snow, but it was too late to do anything about it. We made our way inside.

We got in and immediately looked around for somewhere to hide. The crisp smell and warm air inside were a relief. One lone cashier stood behind a plexiglass shield. Thankfully, they weren't paying much attention to the people who came in. Morris noticed a restroom at the far end of the building. We headed in and locked the door. Morris grabbed his phone and tapped around until I heard a chime sound echo off the bathroom walls. "OK, we got lucky. We got a driver that can be here in 7 minutes," he said.

I looked in the mirror above the bathroom

sink and saw that I still had blood on me from the accident. I turned on the water and grabbed one of the paper towels from the dispenser next to me. The cold water woke me up a little as I brushed the wet paper towel over my face. Drops of red dripped into the sink and trickled into the drain. I watched the blood trace down the sink like the melted snow on the window. After what felt like a couple of minutes, Morris' phone dinged.

"OK, they're almost here. Let's go," he said as he swung the restroom door open. We stepped out and quickly marched toward the gas station entrance. After just a few steps, we heard a police radio. The police officer from the accident was standing by the door. He peered around looking down the aisles to find us. We heard his heavy boots coming in our direction. We quickly ducked down out of sight. My body panged a little from demanding so much movement too soon.

We stayed low and waited to see the officer get closer. As soon as he did, we quietly darted around the other side and just missed him. Tiptoeing as quietly as we could the rest of the way, we eventually reached the entrance. I made the mistake of looking at the cashier, who looked back at me, puzzled. We rushed through the doors before he had the time to put anything together. We leaped into the back of the rideshare and slammed the door shut.

We ducked low in the back seat as the car pulled away from the gas station. It pulled around the blocked-off area of the accident and through the street.

"Where are we on time?" I asked.

"About an hour," replied Morris, "A little less."

I took a labored deep breath and prepared myself for what could be next.

CHAPTER 13

"I think people calm down by breathing because it reminds them that they are still alive. It tells them that they are still in control of something. When we breathe, we fill our bodies with existence. It steadies the mind from the chaotic swaying of constant movement between life and death. Winter is especially harsh, so it has to physically show us the breath coming from within us.

It also puts us all on common ground. Even the evilest of evil breathes in the same breath we have to. We're all down here on two legs trying to keep our lungs protected. It's the first thing they check when a baby is born and the final indicator that you are no longer allowed to be humanized when you die. Something about taking deep breaths starts things over."

//

We walked into the record store, and it was extremely underwhelming. I'd never been there before, but it was a pretty regular looking place. No cauldrons. No floating ghost employees. Not even spiderwebs in the corners. Everything I had pictured in my mind on the way there had faded from my thoughts at the sight of the store. The realization of showing up there started to feel more and more like a mistake the longer I looked around. I was scared. Embarrassed. But the large record player lighthouse logo they had on the wall behind the checkout counter gave me hope.

"OK, so... what do we do?" Morris asked. I didn't answer right away. I didn't really know. I took a second to look around some more. Keyboards, guitars, and other instruments lined the walls. There were crates full of vinyl records up and down the store's aisles. Rarer records were in glass cases by the checkout area. But not a book in sight. I examined the doors on both sides of the protruding wall behind the registers. Before I could get too far in my thoughts, someone came through the one on the right side with a cart of items.

My heart began to sink. I couldn't accept the thought that the trip was all for nothing. I kept telling myself there had to be something there. I scanned every inch of the store looking for anything, absolutely anything. My search was interrupted by one of the employees walking up to us.

"Can I help you find anything?" she pleasantly asked.

"No, we're just looking. Thanks," I replied, not making eye contact with her.

"OK, no problem! Just let us know if you need anything."

She headed back towards the checkout area

when a customer called her over to them. Her kind tone increased my doubts. I couldn't imagine her being the kind of person that would suck the soul out of someone for her own gain. "Braxton, I don't know, man," Morris said. "I don't think this was it." His disappointment sent sadness through my whole being.

I took one more desperate look around the store. Hoping that anything, *anything*, would stick out to me. After not being able to bare it any longer, I slowly headed back toward the exit. Uncontrollable tears began to run down my face as I pushed through the door. *"I really thought this was it. Nothing else makes sense,"* I thought. But then I remembered none of this *really* made sense. The more I thought about it, the more I wanted to detach from reality. I looked over at Morris, who seemed to be letting me have a private moment.

"Sorry, man," I managed to finally say.

"Sorry for what?" he asked, puzzled.

"Sorry for dragging you all the way out here for nothin' and spending all your mon-"

"You're not *dragging* me anywhere," Morris interrupted. "I came here on my own. And I got plenty of money, Braxton. Besides, don't forget that we're out here to save your *life*. Don't think that's 'nothin'."

He lightly patted me on the back and walked towards the parking lot. Morris took out his phone to order a ride. But something didn't feel right. I wouldn't have considered myself the stubborn type, but just leaving the record store, leaving there after all that had happened that day, just didn't sit well with me.

"Wait," I blurted, walking over to Morris. He waited patiently for me to tell him what I had in mind. I waited patiently to discover it. I started to examine the area we were in. He stood up straight from leaning against the handicap parking sign in the parking lot. After a couple of moments, he helped me look around for anything else. Maybe out of curiosity. Maybe out of pity.

I notice a narrow pathway on the side of the building that led to the rear. "Let's see if there's anything back there," I suggested. Morris silently agreed and followed me to the back of the building. Hope rose again within me. Partially from desperation. But I was willing to try anything.

There wasn't a whole lot in the back of the building. A snow-filled dumpster. Some unkempt shrubbery. Boxes. Unfortunately, nothing eventful. "What about this?" Morris asked. I looked in his direction, and he was pointing at a rusty emergency exit ladder that led to the top of the building.

"What about it?" I asked curiously.

"Let's see where it goes," Morris replied.

"It goes to the top of the building."

"I know that, fool. What's up *there*?"

I walked over towards the ladder. I lightly pushed him out of the way and interlocked my fingers to give him a boost up to grab the formally red ladder. Morris placed his wet, snowy boot into my hand. The slush at the bottom squashed between my fingers. I lifted him up as much as I could. It was barely enough, but after a little straining, Morris grabbed the bottom rung of the ladder and leaped down. The snow-covered ladder rumbled and plummeted to the ground. The quiet area gave a more dramatic echo than necessary. Morris let me get a few steps ahead and then followed after me. I quickly realized I had never climbed a ladder before. After a paced climb, we got to the top.

The whole roof was covered in a thick layer of untouched snow. Although the building wasn't extremely tall, the view showed more than I expected. I'd never seen Midland from that angle before. Another first for the day. I wasn't as scared of heights as I imagined I'd be. I carefully looked over the side to where we had just come from and saw our footprints leading toward the back of the building. Bellows of thin smoke rushed out of the store's heating system. There was nothing helpful. I checked with Morris before diving any lower into hopelessness.

"I don't see anything. Do you?" I asked.

"Nah. Nothin'," he replied softly.

After another quick look at the city, I headed back to the ladder. The regret kept my head down.

Morris followed behind in silence. Suddenly, I heard him trip and fall. "Ow! Bleep!" he shouted. I walked over to help him up, assuming he slipped or something. He brushed the snow from the rooftop, trying to figure out what he tripped over. That's when we realized he didn't just slip. It was something else. I helped clear the snow from the surface and discovered it was some sort of hatch. Morris sat up and helped me wipe off the rest of the snow.

"What *is* this?" Morris asked.

"This looks like a way in," I replied. "But I checked the entire place. This opening wasn't in the store."

"What? How can it be here and not go into the store?"

"I don't know, but I have to go. But I have to see where it goes."

I grabbed both sides of the hatch and pulled it up. It was dark and hard to look through, even with the bright light from the outside shining in. I climbed inside and was met with a tight-spiraling staircase. Morris climbed in after me and slowly lowered the hatch back down. The outside winds hushed as the hatch closed. We crept down the stairs until we saw a door.

I very slowly leaned my ear against it to see what I could hear. I could faintly pick up the sound of alternative music playing. "This must be the left door that I saw in the store," I whispered to Morris. I couldn't see the other door from the side we were on at the end of the stairs.

They were made to look like they went to the same back area, but they didn't. I recognized that if you walk forward a bit and turn to the right from the store's left door, there was a short path that led to another set of stairs that cut back to the right of us. It went down into a dimly lit area. I could feel myself trembling, but it gave me hope. I quickly became convinced there weren't just records there.

I silently gave Morris the universal "shhh" sign. He nodded. We quietly went down the small path, turned, and walked down the long, dimly lit set of stairs. We got to the door and paused for a second.

"Do we just go in?" Morris whispered. "We

have no clue what's on the other side."

"We can't just *not* go in," I said, trying to convince myself as well.

I grabbed the doorknob and took a deep breath. *"This is it. This has to be it,"* I thought. I turned the knob and slowly pushed the door open. Heat washed over me as I stood to meet my fate at the door.

But nothing happened. The smell of a basement rushed into us and filled the area we were standing in. We walked in, waiting to be attacked by whatever was there. Morris reached back and closed the door behind us, making it all real for me. We stood still for a while to examine the premises with our hearing. Silence. The path of the area took us to the left, so we cautiously followed it until we reached a dark open room in front of us.

I patted around the rocky wall before fully entering and felt a gritty light switch. I flipped it, and torches spread in different spots of the room lit up. When the room brightened, I finally saw something that made sense. A room full of books. A sigh of relief sprinted out of me. I looked back at Morris, who was looking around the room, grinning from ear to ear. Before I got too caught up in emotion, I reminded myself that not only did I need to hurry, but the room was *full* of books.

"OK," Morris started, seemingly reading my mind. "I'll take the left side, and you take the right." There was no reason to argue. I headed to the right side of the room and started looking around. But then, one blaring fact came racing back to my mind: We had no clue what we were looking for. I started searching for anything I could find that even remotely seemed like it could be the book we were looking for. All the books seemed to be copies of the same thing. I picked them all up one by one, flipping through the pages to see if I could see anything that stood out.

The books were odd. I saw pictures of creatures I'd never seen before. Pictures of brains and hearts split in half. There were a few of naked people with their arms in the air, detached from their bodies. But nothing about the fruit. I looked over my shoulder at Morris, who didn't seem to have found anything, either.

I stepped back for a second to look at the shelves. Nothing stood out. I started to get worried. Every second we spent in the dusty library of nonsense was another second I couldn't use to get the situation over with. I began to think I should have done a better job of asking Nikki about the book. I didn't expect there would be so many to look through. There had to have been thousands of books down there. I wanted to ask Morris what time it was, but I was scared to hear the answer. I could hear him getting frustrated. The books were plopping down harder and faster every minute. After looking through about twenty or so more books, I couldn't resist any longer.

"Where are we on time?" I asked cringingly.

Morris threw the book he was holding into his pile and grabbed his phone from his pocket. He looked at all the books left and then at me. His face told it all.

"We got 11 minutes left," he replied. His

voice cracked as the words came from him. I could see he was sad but wanted my approval to display it or not. I don't say a word. I quickly turned around to rummage through the remaining books in front of me. We both went into hyperdrive. I started grabbing books off the shelves as fast as I could. This time, we were barely looking at them. After a page or two, we tossed them on the floor, already holding the next one before the previous one hit the ground.

My heart started to race. Beads of sweat trickled down my body. I thought about what would actually happen if we didn't find the book fast enough. The fear of the unknown rose within me and started to drown me. I didn't want to believe that after everything that happened, we would still lose. We had gotten so far for absolutely nothing. My arms were growing heavy. I could feel my energy start to taper off.

My stomach was tightening up. Queasiness grew worse with every passing second. I just wanted it all to be over. The idea of fighting against the inevitable became heavier in my mind. Tears of panic blanketed my eyes, blurring everything in front of me. Blinking them away was too much of a fight. Too much of a declaration of hope. Any courageousness I had within me became embarrassed of me and retreated. Then, seconds before I fully withdrew inwardly, I pulled one of the books and the shelves started to split apart.

I lifted my hand and realized the book I had just pulled activated some sort of secret door. Before I had time to react, a blood-curdling scream came from behind the bookshelves.

"What in the hot hell is that?" Morris shouted with his hands over his ears.

"I don't know!" I shouted back as loud as I could over the scream.

The shriek cloaked the entire room. I fell onto the mountain of books I made behind me. The sharp pain in my ears gave me chills. I tried to leverage myself with the books under me but slipped. The heap dissipated as the splitting shelves pushed some of the books on the bottom out of the way. I pushed myself off the pile and stood in front of the entranceway that was in front of me. The screaming got more intense, seemingly quaking the walls. I pushed past the noise and walked into the lit entrance. Then, I saw it.

The *book*.

It sat nestled in a carved space of a large dying tree. Its cover was the bark from the tree and it blended in, almost looking like part of it. The tree sat in grayish soil that looked wet and dry all at the same time. Growing from the tree was the strange fruit. The branches were pumping slowly into the fruits that dangled from them. A blue liquid pulsated throughout the entire tree, illuminating the room's otherwise dark area. The beautiful sight momentarily took my mind away from why we were there. I shook myself out of the thought and looked back, who Morris was still on the floor covering his ears.

"Morris! Morris, I found it!" I yelled to him.

"Yea, I see that!" he replied.

I grabbed the book from within the tree. Its weight caught me off guard. I ran over to Morris and dragged him up by the arm. "We gotta get out of here! Now!" I shouted. We both ran through the opening to the room, through the door we came through earlier, and back up the dark narrow stairs.

I tried to squeeze the book tightly against me to dampen the sound as we went past the left door to the record store. It didn't seem to help. We raced up the spiral staircase to get back to the hatch. Before we could make it all the way up, we heard the hatch slam shut above us. We looked up and saw Dr. Coleman at the top of the staircase.

"No!" he growled as he looked at me clinching the book. His yellowish eyes shined in the dark area. Dirty fog poured from his nostrils as he partially transformed again. He gritted his teeth in anger. Morris and I backed up, almost tripping over each other to get away. Morris yanked open the door we passed to the record store and plowed through it. I immediately followed him.

"Come here!" Dr. Coleman yelled. He charged down the staircase after us. People stared at us, gasping, as we are racing through the store. I heard Dr. Coleman's footsteps march behind us.

Morris reached the entrance of the store first. He tucked himself into his shoulder and blasted into the door, not interrupting his stride. We made it outside, but Dr. Coleman, and now the three of the store employees, were chasing after us. We kept moving forward until we were at the end of the parking lot when suddenly, Nikki pulled up right in front of us.

"Get in!" she shouted. Morris snatched open the car door and jumped in almost completely horizontally. I followed right behind him. Nikki hit the gas and sped off before the car door even shut. We looked through the back window and saw our pursuers looking at us at the end of the record store parking lot.

"I got to mom's, and you weren't home, so I freaked out!" shouted Nikki over the roar of her engine.

"Yo, that was that doctor from the hospital!" Morris yelled.

"Forget them!" Nikki demanded. "Find what you have to do in that book!"

I opened the screaming book and flipped

through the pages for any instructions on what to do. I quickly turned page after page after page until I found one with something that looked like what the woman from the video had mentioned. There were a few words under the pictures that weren't in English. I took my finger and followed along the letters saying them out loud the best I could:

"Nakiri kwamba mwanga ni wa juu Zaidi"

"Nakiri kwamba mwanga ni wa juu Zaidi"

"Nakiri kwamba mwanga ni wa juu Zaidi"

I shouted the words at the top of my lungs. As soon as I said them the third time, the book stopped screaming. "What happened? What's going on?" she asked anxiously. I didn't know what to say. Before I could answer, I burst out in hot, bitter tears. Slamming the book shut, I placed my forehead against the rough cover and cried harder than I have ever cried before. I wept uncontrollably until the little that was still in me was empty.

"Ay," Morris said tapping me on the arm.

I look up at him to see what he wanted. He turned his phone towards me so I could see the time.

It was 6:59 pm.

CHAPTER 14

"Peace. That's all I'm thinking about today. Peace."

//

The following morning was the first time I remember ever being happy to wake up. I sat up in bed and took the time to appreciate the sunlight beaming through the room's dirty curtains. The dust and pollen wafted through the air in front of me like I was in an ocean of it. Genie had already been up watching TV, talking to the characters on his show through the screen. I rolled out of bed and hugged Genie. It surprised both of us. But we didn't care. "I'm the red one!" he shouted in excitement, pointing at the television. I patted him on the shoulder and headed to the bathroom. My back was still sore from getting beat the night before for coming home so late, but daydreams of how the day went before helped with the pain.

My mind transported me again to all the new worlds I got to see. Morris's house was my favorite. I had never felt what a home was like until I went there. I wondered what that refrigerator did. What his mom and dad were like. And his sisters. My thoughts carried me over to the break room at Nikki's job. She had never told me about it before. Maybe because she knew I wouldn't be able to go.

I left the bathroom and went to the kitchen where Nikki was cooking something on the stove. Seeing her face yet again reminded me of how grateful I was for her. I went over to her to say something about yesterday, but my mother burst from her room unexpectedly. She glared at me as she waddled past me to the bathroom. When it felt safe, I redirected my attention back to Nikki.

"Yo," I said, looking in her skillet.

"Ay," she replied with a smile.

Our greetings were minimal but heartfelt.

"I still can't believe all that is over," I murmured cautiously.

"Yea, I bet you're glad. That was crazy," she laughed.

I gave her all the details of the things she wasn't aware of. She seemed impressed that I had gotten as far as I did. I kept telling her that Morris did all the work, but she wouldn't accept that. I didn't care who got the glory. I was just glad it was over with. Out of everything that went down, the weirdest thing that happened was my desire to mean something. I came to the conclusion before going to bed that I wanted to figure out what I wanted to do with my life. Find my purpose. I began to believe I could do a lot more than what I had been doing. I was taking life for granted for so long. I had to change that.

I heard the toilet flush and tried to look busy, hoping my mother would leave me alone. I thanked God that she was leaving for work. "You better not pull that mess you again yesterday again, boy!" she shouted on her way out of the front door. I looked at her to show an acknowledgment. The house shook as she slammed the door behind her.

"I go in late today, so I can give you and Genie a ride to school," Nikki said.

"Thanks!" I replied.

Music to my ears.

We quickly ate breakfast. Eggs and ground beef with a "morning seasoning" Nikki stole from her job. There wasn't a lot of food but I was still grateful to eat something warm before school. After we finished, we piled into Nikki's car. Genie peered out of the window for his friends down the street, then got distracted with himself fogging up the glass, proceeding to draw in it. It was so good to not have to stand in the cold and rush to school for the first time in a while.

We dropped off Genie first and then headed to

my school. In the car, we didn't say much. The music filled the gaps in random sentences. I looked around at all the stuff I didn't get a chance to see often. Nikki let me sightsee for a little while but then decided to check on me when we were almost at the school.

"You sure you're OK? I can call you out today if you want." Nikki said.

"Yea, I'm good. I'm sure I got a lot to catch up on from yesterday," I replied.

I opened the car door to get out. Nikki grabbed the back of my coat.

"Love you, Hicks," she said softly.

"Love you too," I replied, taking one last moment to glance at her before leaving.

I got out of the car and saw that I was definitely early. Even Morris wasn't there yet. I put my bag on the snowy ground and sat on top of it. I waited around, watching people trickle in here and there between daydreams. No one seemed to care that I was there. I liked it that way. Eventually, Morris' parents pulled up in a sleep black luxury car. It somehow looked great even in the wintertime. I tried to get a glance at his parents but could not see through the tinted windows.

"Yo! What up, man?" he shouted as he walked up.

I got up, grabbed my bag, and shook the snow off.

Yo!" I replied.

Our handshake seemed to be more spirited than usual.

"Anything crazy last night?"

"Nah. Not one thing."

"Nice!"

We watched the school guard walk his usual routine of standing by the set of doors at the entrance of the school until the exact minute he was supposed to. After he finally let us in, we wandered inside the cafeteria so Morris could get his daily cinnamon toast fix. The same regulars were there. Some kids were eating, but a lot of people just sitting around talking. I followed Morris into the food line and watched him flirt with the lunch ladies. They just laughed and gave him his toast and milk. He was pretty much a celebrity at the school. We ended up at a table near the exit to the hallway.

"I slept like a baby last night," Morris said, opening his milk.

"Yea, me too," I lied. I had to clean the bathroom most of the night.

"Did you bring it?"

"Bring what?"

Morris leaned in toward me and looked around.

"The book, fool!"

"Oh! Yea, it's in my bag," I nudged my head toward the bag next to me.

"Did you read any more of it?"

"Nah. Didn't really have time."

"Don't tell Mrs. Cunningham you said that."

After we talked for a while, the bell rang, and we made our way to the first class of the day. We got to the classroom and saw that Mr. Fredrickson had returned. I heaved my bag off my shoulder and placed it on the floor under my desk. Slowly, the classmates started to come in, and the start bell for 1st hour rang. A couple of kids darted into the room and ran to their seats. After a few chuckles, Mr. Fredrickson began his lesson. I leaned over to Morris when the coast was clear.

"Ay," I said cautiously.

"Yo," he replied.

"I kinda don't know what to do with this book,"

"I thought about that too. What *could* you gonna do with it?"

"I'm not sure, either. Maybe burn it or somethin'. I don't know."

"*Burn* it? I don't know about that. Have you seen movies? Bad idea."

"I'm not sure, then. I real-"

Mr. Fredrickson almost caught us, but we played it off well enough to continue our conversation. "I really don't want to be walking around with it," I said. A few minutes passed as we camouflaged ourselves as focused students, thinking about what to do with the book. I had never really thought too far ahead about the whole thing. Morris apparently hadn't either. But, I couldn't walk around with it forever.

Mr. Fredrickson looked like he saw us but, to my surprise, he didn't say anything. We decided to play it safe for a while and stay quiet. The last thing I wanted was to get separated. My mind drifted for the majority of the class. But after a while, for once, I actually found myself paying attention to what Mr. Fredrickson was saying.

"There are a lot of quotes from him that have shaped me," Mr. Fredrickson said, pacing in front of the classroom. "I always say if the lesson didn't cost anything, it wasn't a lesson. And he definitely paid the cost. The controversies he endured spanned for years. Even to the discontinuation and banning of his published literature."

He took a coin out of his pocket and held it up for the class to see. He stood there for a moment, examining the coin. "One of my favorite quotes," he continued, "is *Due verita non possono contraddirsi i'una con l'altra,'* which translates in English to 'Two truths cannot contradict one another.'. Let's think about it for a moment, shall we?" He put the old coin away in his vest pocket.

"What you believe and what I believe can't coexist if they are opposing matters. For instance, if you believe there is only one God, and I believe that there are many gods, one of us *has* to be wrong. Or I say, 'We are all royalty.' and you say 'No, we are all to be servants.', again, one of us *must* be incorrect. There is no such thing as 'your truth' or 'my truth'. Only fact and opinion."

Mr. Fredrickson paused, seemingly digesting his words. He stilled himself, almost becoming a statue right in front of us. Then, with just his eyes moving, he looked directly at me. Practically *into* me. I froze in my seat. My mouth started getting extremely dry, and I got hot all over. Without budging his gaze, he continued. "Or... when someone says *'Nakiri kwamba mwanga ni wa juu Zaidi.,'* I would tell them darkness reigns supreme."

I could almost feel the ghost rise out of my body. My whole being froze stiff. My hands rattled hard on my desk. Suddenly, the bell rang. But I couldn't move. Mr. Fredrickson had a grip on my presence and wouldn't let go. Students began to file out of the room. The room was filled with the sound of desks moving around. All sound was muffled besides the rusty weighted breathing of Mr. Fredrickson.

It was like he was in my head. I could nearly hear him growling from inside me. Soon, the room was empty besides me, Morris, and Mr. Fredrickson. "We shall feast on the blood from your skull, Boy of Midland," he hissed, sinisterly.

Morris snatched me out of my desk, and we run out of the classroom as fast as our fear allowed. I looked back at Mr. Fredrickson, who had his head turned toward us but his body in the same position. He smiled a vicious and humanly impossible smile as saliva dripped slowly down his lips onto his desk. Morris and I ran down the hallway until we were far from the classroom.

"Yo! What was that?" Morris yelled.

"I don't know!" I replied.

My mind wouldn't allow me to comprehend

what happened. I knew I had definitely said the words from the book. I said them over and over. I had to have done all that right, or I'd be dead. There was a tornado of confusion, fear, and worry in my head. Every second it got harder not to throw up. "I thought this was done," I said. "We followed all the instructions from the video. We found the book and said the words. What else could there be?" Morris just stood in silence as my words fell flat on the ground. We didn't know what to do, so we went to the only person I could trust.

"Guys, I don't have time for this," Mrs. Cunningham said, shuffling papers around on her desk. Students for her next class came in one by one and sat at their desks.

"Mrs. Cunningham, *please*! I know this sounds crazy, but we don't know what to do!" Morris replied. She was not budging.

"Morris Wilson, I *know* you are behind all this and somehow talked Braxton into helping you do whatever it is you're doing, but I will not let you get him or myself involved."

"Mrs. Cunningham, I know I play around a lot, bu-" Morris pleaded. Mrs. Cunningham slammed her papers on her desk and glared at both of us.

"Do *not* say another word to me, or I'll walk you to in-house myself. Now, both of you need to leave. Now."

We quietly made our way out of Mrs. Cunningham's classroom. A few of the kids tried to hide their stares as they watched us leave. The only hope we had was now gone.

"*Now* what?" I asked Morris, who had started to panic as badly as I was.

"I don't know, man. There's no way to skip this early and not get caught. Even if we did, I don't know where to go."

We lingered into one of the bathrooms down the hall from Mrs. Cunningham's class. A couple of people shuffled out, and soon after, we heard the bell ring to be in 2nd hour. We paced around and tried to figure out what we would do next. "What is happening?" Morris asked. "I don't get it. The video said to find the book, say the words, and everything would be fine. How did Mr. Fredrickson find out what we did? How was he looking like that?" I was at a loss for words.

Morris leaned against the side panel of one of the stalls. I searched my mind for answers. Any answers at all. I was almost nauseous. I went inside one of the bathroom stalls and locked the door. I got on my knees and put my head in the toilet to throw up. The smell of urine and feces rushed up to me. I hovered over the bowl for a while, looking for any way out. Then, we heard a tin voice behind the bathroom door.

"Braxton Tatum, report to the main office, please. Braxton Tatum, to the main office. Thank you."

I shot up from the floor and darted out of the stall to confirm what I heard with Morris. He was standing there with wide eyes and his mouth open. We froze for a moment, wanting the voice to have been muffled enough to question it. But we both knew it wasn't. "I can't go to the office," I said. Morris shook his head in agreement. I crept to the exit of the bathroom. Very slowly, I opened it and peeked out into the hallway to see if anyone was close by. No one seemed to be in range.

"We gotta get out of here," I whispered to Morris.

"And go where?" he replied.

"I don't know, but it's only a matter of time before they're in here checking these bathrooms for me."

I swung the door open, continuing to check around, and proceeded down the hall. I heard Morris shuffle behind me. I didn't know what to do, so I rummaged through my mind for a solution. I felt my head starting to hurt. My body got hotter and hotter with each passing second. "Let's go to the gym," Morris suggested. "It's big enough to run if we get caught.

I didn't give it a second thought. We flung around corners and under staircases until we made it to the school gymnasium. I headed in and looked around. Everyone was scattered throughout, slowly coming out in ones and twos from the boy's locker room. "In there," I whispered to Morris. He nodded. We flattened against the walls until we got to the locker room's entrance.

The gym was shaped like a colosseum. Once you walked in, the main, or "upper", level had a medium-sized hardwood running track with a few doors that lined the walls leading to the halls of the school. In the center was the lower level. The lower level was a large hardwood floor scribbled with markings from different sports. There was a way to the floor by any of four sets of stairs in each corner of the level.

After a quick glance, it looked like everyone was preoccupied on the lower level, so we made it inside the locker room unseen. When we got inside, the smell of sweat and damp heat demanded our attention. It was a reasonably large room with four rows of medium-sized dark blue lockers stacked on one another that drug your eyes to the dingy marble-looking light blue floor. Behind the row of lockers, there was an office. We headed in that direction.

Right when we were almost there, the locker

room door opened behind us. Morris and I split apart and stood up against an end of the locker aisles away from the door. I tried to ease my panicked breathing to be as quiet as possible. The person that came in slowly took a couple of steps inside. The sound of the lockers opening and closing next to us got closer with each time we heard it.

My mind was racing as the footsteps approached us. Suddenly the locker room door opened again. I heard frantic steps rush inside and then back out. A locker door quickly slammed shut, startling me. Then I heard someone on the other side of the door yell, "See? Look, y'all! I finally caught him stealin'!" The person in the room with us ran to the door. "Nuh uh! I was looking for something!" he replied. The open door revealed the sound of a few other people nearby. A cloud of threats and curse words grew larger until the thunderous voice of Ms. Lee broke it up. "Get back down here! Now!" The leftover voices continuously lessened, eventually returning to quiet.

I exhaled the breath I didn't know I was

holding. I looked over at Morris, who was just about to say something when we heard someone come into the locker room again. I snapped back into the position I was in before. The person seemingly paced back and forth in the room. My legs were getting tired from standing so stiff, but I pushed through the urge to move. After a few more seconds, we heard the person's phone dialing out. I funneled my hearing to listen. "It's a negative here," the person said.

It was Ms. Lee. I wanted to relax when I heard the familiar voice, but I didn't risk it. I needed to find out how many of the teachers were like Mr. Fredrickson. She continued talking to the mystery voice. "They swept the surrounding area, and I was advised that there is no sign of him. OK. Will do. OK. Bless Stellan." Ms. Lee ended the call and walked out of the locker room. We waited for a couple of seconds before moving too soon. When we felt it was safe, we continued our route to the dark office. Morris looked mortified.

We sat in a corner with our backs against the wall. I took the book out of my bag and stared at it. It was odd to believe that something I held in my hands held so much power. I opened it, flipping through the pages for anything that could make sense of what was happening. Morris moved over to help look. I angled the pages closer to the light of the locker room. I looked through a few pages but decided to give myself a moment to think. Closing my eyes, I leaned my head back against the filing cabinet next to me. It felt like the more I wanted to know, the more confusing things got, so pausing for a moment felt better than searching for answers. "What are we gonna do?" I asked Morris desperately. He didn't respond.

After sitting there for a few minutes, the lights in the locker room unexpectedly shut off The hum from the fluorescent lights faded away and turned the atmosphere to still silence. The sound of voices on the outside of the room could faintly be heard. I got up from the floor and peered into the dark locker room. "What's goin' on?" Morris asked. Then the tin voice of the intercom returned.

"Attention students and faculty. There has

been a school-wide power outage due to severe weather conditions. Please remain in your classrooms until further notice. The city has been notified, and they have advised that they will be getting us back up and running as soon as possible. Due to safety and security reasons, no one other than school personnel is allowed outside of the classrooms at this time. All current school policies are still intact. Teachers, please contact the main office if there are any questions. Thank you."

The weather had been the same for the past week. I knew what that was.

I was being hunted.

CHAPTER 15

"Worry is blindness. I've worried about a lot in my fifteen years of life. Nothing comes from worry but creative imaginary scenarios. Day by day, another room of your mind gets filled with screams of fake blood and panic. With each minute, you borrow heartbeats from the future to hand over to the characters you created in your mind's presentation. No moment is unblemished. Worry is like a thick spiderweb you can see through but can't make out what you're looking at. Worry is blindness."

//

"We gotta get out of here," Morris said, turning on the flashlight on his phone.

"I know," I replied.

"No, we gotta get out of *here*."

"I *know*, Morris!"

I helped him search the area for a way out. I knew it was going to be difficult. Not that it wasn't hard before. The beings behind all this were searching for me, and they would eventually get to the office we were in. At that point, we were going to have to try to get out of the school entirely. There didn't seem to be any other way out besides the way we came in. We weren't sure if we could just run or not. The dark could be of some use. The gym was somewhat noisy. The students were definitely being more quiet than usual, though. Either way, there was no point in just standing there.

"We have to just go," I said.

"Just... walk out?".

"Yea. I mean, what else is there?"

After a hurried reexamining of the dark room, Morris agreed. We established a path to the door with his flashlight before turning it off. A couple of deep breaths calmed us before we crept toward the exit. I slowly opened the door, cautious not to make any noise doing so. I looked back at Morris to make sure he was still OK. He seemed to be as nervous as I was. Right when we were about to step through, the silhouette of Ms. Lee walked in front of us in the doorway.

Ms. Lee walked into the dark locker room. She looked into me and grinned happily. She walked closer toward us as we backed up until the door shut behind her. I heard Morris fearfully moving around behind me. As the book shut, the dark locker room became pitch black in front of me. Then I saw the illuminating yellowish eyes of Ms. Lee. "Hello, Boy of Midland!"

Morris screamed, and I punched Ms. Lee in the eye. A tint of blue flashed onto her face as I hit her. I stumbled over Morris, trying to back away. Ms. Lee grabbed my shirt and pulled me toward her. A scream came from me when I felt the heat from her breath wrap around my neck and cover me with chills. I tried to pull away, but her grip was too strong.

Then Morris flashed his light in her eyes. He tried to pull me away from her, jerking on my arm as hard as he could. I couldn't seem to keep my footing. I heard my shirt tearing little by little. I kicked Ms. Lee with all my strength on the side of her right knee. She wailed and collapsed to the ground, letting me go to hold her leg. I snatched open the locker room door to get out. It hit Ms. Lee in the side of the head as we squeezed through the opening, knocking her unconscious.

We bolted out and ran to the exit of the gym we used to come in earlier. The hallway seemed longer since we couldn't see anything. The echoes of our panting engulfed the area around us. We ran toward the set of double doors leading to the entrance of the school. We checked the area through the narrow glass above the push bar on the doors. No one seemed to be in sight.

I quietly pushed the door open and entered the area. We tiptoed toward the side exit of the school but quickly aborted once we saw a guard near us looking for me. We changed direction and took refuge under a set of stairs to the left a little further down. We pressed in as deep as we could to make sure we couldn't be seen. It was uncomfortable, but it seemed like the safest place to hide.

"Did you see Ms. Lee? That was nuts!" Morris said frantically.

"Yea. Another one," I replied.

Faint footsteps came and went in the distance. The guard we saw came inside the door, and we heard the metal of the frame clamp shut. Walkie Talkies blurted statuses that rippled through the hallway. They were growing more and more frustrated. It felt like we'd been running all day. I knew running and hiding weren't gonna last forever, but I didn't know what else to do. At some point, Ms. Lee was going to be conscious again.

Morris took his phone out, shielding the light with his hand to soften the glow. He turned the brightness down and tried to load something on the screen. It went blank. He kept trying until he realized there was no phone signal. "I always have signal at school," Morris mumbled. He restarted his phone a couple of times and got the same result. He thought for a minute and finally concluded that something was wrong.

"They've done something to block the signals on the phones." I started to panic internally but kept my composure. I was beginning to realize how big this was going to be. I didn't know what to say, so I stayed silent. I didn't want to pass on my worry, but I was sure Morris was starting to feel it too.

I peeked around the stairwell. I still couldn't see much besides the slight shine of the white snow available through the foyer. The guard seemed to have stopped moving as much. We needed a major distraction. The dark seemed to amplify the silence. Even the faintest sounds pulsed through the empty school hallways. I tried to use this to our advantage.

"What if we split up?" I asked.

"What? We've talked about the whole movie

thing, right?" Morris replied.

"Well, we can't just sit here like goofies. If we run in separate directions, they can't catch both of us."

"Yes, they can. They're patrolling the whole school. And when Ms. Lee gets up, it's a wrap. We're done for."

"Which is why we need to go. I'll go this way."

I pointed toward the hallway on the left of us. I knew down that hall and around the corner was the front exit of the school. I was sure it was being guarded, though. But if there's only one guard, we could maybe attack them like we did Ms. Lee. Morris nudged me out of my thinking.

"I'll go," he said quietly.

"What do you mean?" I said, puzzled.

"I mean, I'll run off and make a distraction. Then you can make it outside."

"Morris, you don't have to do that. I-"

"Bruh," he interrupted. "It's cool. We got it."

I paused for a moment. The situation's gravity

pressed me on me inwardly. But before I got the chance to react, Morris sprung up and bolted up the staircase we are hiding under. The air around me got hot with fear. A guard shouted out to Morris and started chasing him. The guard's heavy boots kept in step with my heartbeat as he raced toward the sound. The echoes from Morris and the guard interrupted each other.

When I heard the guard make it to the top of the stairs, I peeled from the shadows and hurried to the side door he was watching over. The sweat all over me chilled as I picked up speed. I rushed as fast as I could to the school exit. I barely made it to the other side of the hallway when I saw a beam of light in front of me.

I whipped my attention to the source and saw one of the guards in the middle of the hallway. "Hey!" he shouted, piercing through my shock. I started to run toward the door. The panic helped my weight take my breath away. The light from the flashlight strobed behind as the guard devoured the space between us. I busted through the metal double doors into the foyer.

The ambiance of the room surrounded me as I paced through the wide area. After a few seconds, the guard charged in after me. I burst through the doors at the other end of the foyer and finally made it outside. The brisk air cooled my sweaty skin. I toward the front of the school to the main street. I could barely breathe. Winter entered my lungs, freezing my insides with each breath. My book bag pounded my back as I pushed closer and closer to the street in front of me.

The grunts from the guard amplified in the quiet morning. I heard him getting closer and closer. My legs began to hurt from the unfamiliar pace. I was about halfway there when I felt the hand of the guard grab my shoulder from behind. I tried to knock his hand off me, but his grip was too strong. I attempted to push him away. I started to tussle with him, but I was too weak from the run. He grabbed me by the arm and dragged me toward the school. "Get *off* of me!" I yelled at the guard. I tried to snatch my arm away with no success. He tugged me aggressively back into his compliance.

"I found him," the guard hollered into his walkie-talkie. I stumbled and slipped trying to pull myself away. With each attempt, the guard squeezed my arm tighter. "Let me go!" I screamed. "Shut up!" The guard replied angrily. His bark seemed to fill the whole space around us. I closed my eyes and tried to focus to bring out the powers I had inside me. I grunted and groaned but couldn't make anything happen. I continued to struggle but couldn't escape.

Suddenly, I heard the door to the school open. Mrs. Cunningham came rushing out towards us. The sound of her high heels broadened out through the air. Her face was fuming. She'd been upset with me before, but I'd never seen her that mad. "What the hell are you doing?" she yelled at the guard, grabbing my other arm to get me away from him. He snatched me back toward him. "I'm doing my job. You should go back inside and do yours," he replied.

Mrs. Cunningham got in his face and screamed at him for a few minutes straight. He eventually threw my arm aside and walked back toward the side door of the school. "This is 804. The kid is now with Pamela Cunningham." He pulled the door open and marched inside.

"Braxton, what is going on? Are you OK?" Mrs. Cunningham asked.

"We need to go get Morris," I answered.

"Morris? What's wrong with Morris?"

I didn't have time to answer. I used the little energy I had left to run back into the school. Mrs. Cunningham followed behind. "Braxton!" she shouted. I didn't even look back. I darted back through the foyer and into the dimmed building. I tried to calm my breathing to listen for Morris running. I couldn't hear anything.

Mrs. Cunningham picked up on what I was doing and stopped to listen with me. The silence was almost sickening. I checked the hiding spot we were in before. Empty. "Morris!" I whispered harshly, hoping the echoes worked with me to find him. "It's me!" I didn't hear the slightest reply. My heartbeat began to pick back up. I looked back at Mrs. Cunningham, who was checking her phone to see if the signal was back. My shaky legs managed to walk back to her.

Before I could find the words to say, she spoke up. "Where did you last see him?" she asked. Her voice was sure and determined. She seemed to not care about staying quiet. I latched on to her bravery. "He wa- we were over there." I pointed toward the crevice under the stairs. "He took off upstairs, and I ran outside." She headed up the wide stairs, searching her phone for the flashlight. The light seemed to illuminate the entire school. "Watch your step," she said, putting her hand on my back. She shined the light on the stairs in front of me.

When we got to the top, the quiet brought on fear. We stood still for a moment to listen for Morris. I got more scared every second. Guilt pressed against me from every direction. Accusations bullied my focus until there was nothing left but blame and pity. Mrs. Cunningham's voice scattered my thoughts. "Check the bathrooms." I followed her directions and walked into the dark boy's bathroom. A bit of natural light filtered through the dirty glass window It was only somewhat helpful. "Morris. Are you there?" I awaited a reply, but the quiet swallowed my sound. I walked back to Mrs. Cunningham. The shake of my head transmitted a disappointing look to her.

"He's gotta be up here somewhere." We headed down the hall, checking every corner we could. It was hard to keep up with Mrs. Cunningham, but I managed. Her heels sent waves throughout the hallway. Right when we started to panic, a slight shift of a shadow in the distance caught our attention. Mrs. Cunningham held her arm out in front of me. I halted and honed my entire being onto the movement. The shadow gradually got larger and was accompanied by the sound of heavy boots.

"Who is that?" Mrs. Cunningham belted, startling me a bit. "There's not supposed to be anyone in these hallways." The figure was silent. That amplified Mrs. Cunningham's curiosity. She fiercely walked toward the shadow. I debated on staying back, but my fear forced my legs to chase behind her light. Before we got too far, the shadowy figure shaped itself into a school guard. And in front of him,

212

Morris.

Relief embraced me. All the loops of worst-case scenarios playing in my mind faded away as my eyes showed me the truth. Mrs. Cunningham sped her pace toward Morris and the guard. I kept up as much as I could. As I got closer, I notice that Morris looked exhausted but also not too happy about the grip on his shoulder. Sweat glistened on his forehead in the light of Mrs. Cunningham's phone. He must have just gotten caught. Once close enough, Mrs. Cunningham grabbed Morris and brought him in toward us.

The guard took a moment to glance at all of us, taking an extra few seconds to look me up and down, and walked away. After a few seconds, he murmured something on his walkie-talkie. He took a glance back at me before melting back into the darkness. His absence snapped me back into reality. I turned around to check on Morris. Mrs. Cunningham was examining him to make sure he wasn't hurt with the light on her phone

"Yo, are you-" she started.

"Yea, I'm good," Morris interrupted, gazing

past Mrs. Cunningham in front of him.

I stayed quiet for a couple of minutes, letting her finish. "We were lookin' all over for you," I said to Morris. I sounded relieved, which came out as an oddly pitched mess. Morris didn't reply. When Mrs. Cunningham felt satisfied with Morris' condition, she silently approved his ability to move forward. I walked over to Mrs. Cunningham. She was checking her phone again for a signal. I didn't know what to say, so I looked up at her, hoping she prompted something. "So. Tell me, gentleman," she said through a surrendering huff. "What's going on?"

We went into the nearby empty computer lab and told her everything. I abandoned all safety and made sure every detail was spewed out in a plain clear fashion. The fruit, the book, the demons, everything. Mrs. Cunningham couldn't believe what she was hearing. Some stuff seemed gentler to swallow than others. I couldn't imagine being the person hearing those things without seeing them.

Just a week ago, I would have thought it was from a movie. It was hard to believe even for me. But we spared no detail. After we went over the whole story, Mrs. Cunningham took a deep breath and stared off into the distance. I looked down at the floor to give her time to process everything we told her.

After a few moments go by, Mrs. Cunningham stood up from the seat she was in. "I think we need to go," she said. I stiffened and widened my eyes at the shock of what she was saying. I looked over at Morris, who seemed to feel the same way. "What do you mean 'go'?" he asked. She opened the door to the lab slowly and listened for any sound. Morris and I are watching her in astonishment. I looked back at her as she was turning around back towards us. "Let's go."

We stood up and followed her out the door. We closed it silently and headed toward the stairs we came up earlier. As we got closer, I heard a slight shuffle below us. We paused to give the silence our undivided attention. The sounds got a bit louder with each second and eventually revealed itself as an assortment of footsteps. We went down the stairs to meet it. We got to the bottom of the dark staircase and were met with the last person I wanted to see.

Ms. Lee.

CHAPTER 16

"Frustration is the scared version of anger. It's reserved for the timid people who know they aren't going to do anything. It allows them to give a physical sign that they're upset while clearly recognizing they aren't pushed to the point of violence. People who are frustrated communicate that they are powerless over their situation and can only be mad about it. It seems like part of the anger is the recognition of their weakness. The inner longing to be the kind of person to go beyond grunting and emotional censorship. But a longing it will remain."

//

"Stop right there!" Ms. Lee yelled out toward us. I walked up a little closer for defiance. Her frail state bred bravery. She stood with two school guards holding her up on each side to keep her from falling over. As I got closer to her, I noticed the streaks of dirt and grime on her face. The gleam of sweat also made itself known with Mrs. Cunningham's light. The guards rebutted the shine with their flashlights pinned to their uniforms. I started to wonder if the guards knew what Ms. Lee really was.

"These two are coming with me," Ms. Lee declared.

"No, they're not," said Mrs. Cunningham, stepping up closer to her.

Ms. Lee's eyes pierced through my entirety. I tried not to move, but I felt myself loosen my stance a bit in nervousness. Her gritted teeth looked as if they wanted to devour me. Mrs. Cunningham quickly pulled me back behind her. Ms. Lee noticed the challenge and motioned the guards to help her move forward. They clinched her arms and pulled her in front of Mrs. Cunningham. Their eyes never unlocked from each other.

"They assaulted me! They will need to deal with the authorities! You can't just attack people and walk away!" Ms. Lee barked.

"It looks like you fell, Barbara," Mrs. Cunningham replied. "You *are* a gym teacher. Accidents happen all the time."

"You know that's not what happened!"

"No, I don't. I was in my classroom until I saw one of the guards harassing a student."

"They attacked me, and they *know* it!"

Ms. Lee forced the words through her teeth. Drops of spit darted past the beams from the flashlights. I could see her losing the little amount of composure she came with. She looked over at me and then at Morris with tamed rage.

"Are you sure it was them?" asked Mrs. Cunningham. Ms. Lee's put her focus back on her. "The lights have been out for some time now. Can you say, without a doubt, that it was them? Can you manage to provide any proof? And besides all that, Barbara, please explain to me why on God's green Earth would two students plan a collaboration to skip class, go to the gym and *beat you up*."

That sent Ms. Lee into a straight up frenzy. The guards who were once there to hold her up were now holding her back. She was kicking the leg she could move and trying to wrestle herself out of the grip of the guards. The echo from her yelling surrounded me and rang in my ears. A couple of other teachers opened their classroom door and peeked down the hall where we were to see what was happening.

"Is everything alright, Pam?" one of them asked from behind us. Mrs. Cunningham gently raised a hand up in response and they quietly returned to their classes. She never lifted her gaze from Ms. Lee. After the two guards drug Ms. Lee further into the darkness and out of sight, the sound of struggle faded with her. Mrs. Cunningham took a soft breath and turned to us. "You boys OK?" she asked, hesitating to force a smile but deciding not to go through with it. Morris and I nodded.

We made our way out of the school and into Mrs. Cunningham SUV. Although there weren't any guards near the door now, I couldn't help but think of how easy it just was to walk out with her with us. I sat in the back this time with Morris. He seemed to be a little bit more spirited. We put our seat belts on and watched Mrs. Cunningham quickly scrap the thin layer of ice off her windshield.

Eventually, notifications from Morris' phone barged through the quiet. I saw Mrs. Cunningham getting hers out as well. For a second, they both transported to a separate consciousness as I waited patiently to exist again. The muffled sound of Mrs. Cunningham making a call disturbed my thoughts. A breeze of words that could've maybe been interpreted as "I love you, too" made me imagine her talking to her husband, Mark.

Mrs. Cunningham got into the now warm car and backed out of the parking lot. She messed around with the radio stations but then decided the radio was unnecessary. I looked for a drop of melted snow to focus on. But I couldn't shake my thoughts. I couldn't get my mind off what just happened.

I felt like I was dragging everyone through so much. I couldn't do anything about it and that made it worse. Feeling like I was being tolerated was so heavy in my mind. I wished I could just run away and deal with whatever this was on my own. Or not deal with it at all. My stomach soured as my mind reminded me how much of a failure I had been.

After a while, we made it to Mrs. Cunningham's house. Her neighborhood looked a lot like Morris'. Clean cut copied & pasted houses. Polite and organized. The car crept into the garage's mouth and swallowed us whole. We got out of the car and were met with a woody, autumn smell. The aroma alone warmed my insides. We stepped into the house after Mrs. Cunningham typed in a code on a panel just inside the doorway.

Her house looked like I had entered a movie set for a family film. The refrigerator was matted with colorful sticky notes, and a scribble-filled dry erase board. The counter looked like something from a cooking show. Her clean floors made me scared to even walk on them. The cautious scent of cinnamon gently introduced itself as we got further into the kitchen. Mrs. Cunningham briefly walked into another room for a few seconds to put her things down, then came back to us.

"You boys hungry?" she said, softly lifting her eyebrows. "Give me a second. I have sandwich stuff in the fridge. There are chips in that cabinet over there. The bread's in there too." She pointed to a polished wood cabinet above the stove. I decided to grab it all so Morris didn't have to worry about it.

Mrs. Cunningham walked back over from her refrigerator and filled the dining room table with more food than I'd seen at once in my whole life. Sliced turkey, ham, salami, chicken, three different kinds of cheese, lettuce, tomato, pickles, and a million different half-empty sauce bottles. "Eat all this because I'm not putting it all back. I have to use the phone," she said, taking a couple of pieces of the ham before marching up her carpeted stairs. Morris and I began our feast.

"I'm gonna make the biggest sandwich known to mankind," Morris said grabbing some bread from the table. "A sandwich so big, I get it for free if I finish it." I picked up the clear glass bottle with a pink and red label that read "Yolanda's Lava Sauce". Morris motioned for it, and I handed it to him. After a lazy investigation of the bottle, he shrugged his shoulders and shook a bunch of it onto his growing sandwich.

"So, what is going on?" he asked. I was hoping to forget about everything for a little while, but I figured it wouldn't last long.

"I don't know," I replied, thinning each word down into an eventual nothing. We sat quietly for a few moments. I reached over and grabbed the bag of chips from the middle of the table. "I need to get this figured out, though," I continued. "I don't want to drag anyone else into-"

"You're not draggin' any of us anywhere, bruh," Morris said. I could sense the sincerity in his voice. "We're here 'cuz we wanna be."

I somehow managed not to choke up. I couldn't help but feel the pressure of everything, killing everybody on the inside. I decided to take his word for it, for now. "Thanks," I said quietly while yelling through the internal storm.

We ate as much as we possibly could and sat back to examine the sandwich-gedon we just committed. I felt like I was going to burst. After a few minutes, Morris brought us back to reality. "Yo, where's that book?" he said curiously. I reached under the table and unzipped my heavy bag. The smell of old pages and dust blended horribly with the kitchen's atmosphere. Being careful not to damage it, I put the book down on the table and stared at it for a moment.

It was definitely the oldest book I had ever seen. The dust and grime in the engravings seemed to belong there. There was no title on the cover. Just a sheet of tree bark covering the whole front of it. I followed the lines of the bark with my eyes until the sound of Morris scooting his chair over disrupted me. I opened the book to the first page, and there were still no words. Only a symbol in the center. The yellowing of the page stopped around the symbol. "What is that?" Morris asked. I shrugged and kept turning the pages, looking for something that made any sense.

Some of the pictures were hard to look at for too long. I shook the images out of my head and kept turning the pages. I wanted the book to shed some light on what was going on, why I was still being chased. I had felt so sure that we did what we were supposed to. Hope faded from me throughout the morning. I didn't understand what was happening. I looked over at Morris, who seemed to be as confused as I was.

I got to the pages that mirrored closely to what Morris and I learned in the video we watched. Chills showered my body as I got a more detailed look. The images paralyzed me. I was shaken back to life by Morris. "You good, bruh?" he asked. His face was scared and concerned. I nodded and slid the book toward him. He pulled it closer to him to get a better look. Suddenly, we heard a faint whimper.

I looked at him and he seemed to have heard it too. I paused for a moment and checked under the table to make sure there weren't any dogs or other animals we didn't see earlier. Nothing. Morris slowly reached out his hand again to touch the book. But that time, I readied myself in my chair and honed my attention to his movements.

His hand slowly hovered over the corner of the page. He tilted his head, slightly pointing one ear towards the book. He lowered his index finger onto the page until he touched the very edge. That time, the whimper was a bit louder. Morris pushed back his chair from the table and stood up. The baffled look on my face confirmed that we weren't crazy.

"Did you hear that? he asked.

"Uh, yea!" I replied.

I examined the book, not sure of what I was looking for. The book's sound had died down to a soft, almost silent, pant. "What just happened?" Morris questioned. I cautiously lowered my hand onto the book's yellowing page. A thin whimper briefly started but stopped almost in the same second.

A relieved sigh came from within the pages. The faint whiff of basements passed by. Without warning from my brain, I softly began to brush my thumb over the aging book. Morris sat back down in his chair. "This has *got* to be a dream," he murmured.

I raised my hand from the book, which seemed to be the calmest thing in the room. I waited a brief moment before I attempted to turn the pages again. When it felt safe to, I continued to search for what to do next. I could make out what some of the pictures described, but some made no sense. I eventually got to a page that showed a weird-looking cave. It was a hub of empty spaces separated by oblong pillars of stone. The web of rooms seemed to span endlessly, fading into darkness as it went on. It resembled bones with osteoporosis that I had seen in Health class. The sporadic pillars looked weak and spongy. The top of the page read "SHIMO LA VITA".

The drawing in the book looked like an abstract painting. It was nothing I had ever seen before. I turned the page, and they explained the area it showed. "The Pit of War," Morris said translating the page on phone. "The room is the key itself. The only entry is an exit. The only exit is an entry. A beginning of ends." Morris said. My face scrunched up at the odd sentence. Morris continued "The room is filled with bloodshed and spiritual anguish. Created through grace for war. Unacceptable in the world it's for."

"Even when you understand this book, it makes no sense," I said.

"I don't get what we're supposed to do with that," Morris replied.

"It's the only thing I've heard so far that has to do with this being over."

"Maybe there's something else."

We searched through the few pages following the odd passage. Nothing seemed to be relevant to what we needed. I went back to the page about The Pit of War. I thought about the words, repeating them in my mind over and over. Before I could think too long about the meaning of the passage, the shuffling of footsteps interrupted me.

Mrs. Cunningham came into the kitchen from upstairs. "Boys," she panted, "It's time to go. Get your things." Morris nervously gathered his stuff. He reached for the bag I had the book in. "Here's I'll take that. Just in case we have to run," he said. I started to hand it to him but felt bad about the burden of being helped. "Nah, it's cool," I replied. He didn't put up much of a fight and headed to the door. I carefully put the book in my bag to keep it from making any noise and followed him. Mrs. Cunningham paused for a second and mumbled a checklist of things she may have needed before leaving. That filled me to the brim with anxiousness. Apparently enough to spill a few words.

"What's goin' on?" I managed to say. Mrs. Cunningham took a deep breath and brought herself back down to Morris and me. "My husband just told me there could be some trouble coming. He drove by the school on his way here from work and he said it looks like there is some commotion on the property. I was telling him what was going on with you and he doesn't know if it's connected but we're just playing it safe."

Relief draped over me. I tried to hide my embarrassment from being so scared. Mrs. Cunningham opened the front door open. The cold air rushed in front of us. "He should be on his way soon," Mrs. Cunningham said as she peered out of the front door. She stepped out of the house to look down the street. As I moved, I started to regret eating so much.

Mrs. Cunningham moved in and out of view. The sound of her heels clicking went up and down every few seconds. After a little while, she came back to the door. "He's pulling up," she said, with a smile. We walked out as she stepped back in to enter the security code on the panel. The sound of slush filled the air as a dark blue sedan pulled up to meet us. The vehicle inched to a stop, easing in close enough to the sidewalk to keep up out of the road.

I got in and slid over as far as I could so Morris could have room. Morris glides in and shuts the door behind him. "What's up, guys?" The driver said, looking at us through the rearview mirror.

Morris and I let out a duo of muffled contrived greetings. "I'm Mark, Pammy's husband,". An encored response from us commenced. "That's 'Mrs. Cunningham' to you until 3:30, young man," Mrs. Cunningham said to Mark, getting in the car and leaning in to kiss him. He smiled and reciprocated. She closed the car door and Mark continued ahead.

The car smelled like cologne. It was well kept and extremely clean. Light jazz music comes from a speaker somewhere near me. Dangling from the rearview mirror was a photo of Mark and Mrs. Cunningham embracing each other on a beach somewhere. The navigation screen scrolled something that I couldn't make out, but I caught myself trying to catch what it said. The warmth of the car soothed me a bit. But then, we heard the explosion.

CHAPTER 17

"There is no such thing as true happiness. There are only the illusions you create for yourself to help you forget that things are going on outside of your life. This world is thick with pain. The first thing babies do when they get here is cry. Out of every possible reaction, crying is what we do naturally.

We get taught at the earliest age to distract. Sleep, eat, play with colorful toys, watch cartoons, go to school, make friends, run around in playgrounds, make friends, create attraction, get married. By the time you have kids, you are a professional at disturbing your conscious truth and can teach it the world's updated version of survival. The more honest you are with yourself, the harder the 'choice' of happiness is. You can either develop yourself through the lessons that honesty presents or play the game."

//

I ducked down in fear of the sound behind us. Mrs. Cunningham gasped as she practically turned all the way around in her seat to watch the huge flames blanket her house. "What the hell was that?" Mark shouted in a rumbled voice. I was too afraid to check but the reflection of the fire on the windshield held me hostage to the image. "That was the house!" Mrs. Cunningham sunk back into her seat.

The whole car was in utter shock. Morris couldn't take his eyes off the scene. I could see him tremoring. I pierced through the fog of panicked voices from the front seat. "We have to go to the hospital!" I blurted out. The car swerved a little. "Are you OK?" Mark asked frantically. His widened eyes filled the rearview mirror. Mrs. Cunningham looked back at me, wiping her tears with a quivering hand. "Are you OK, Braxton? What's wrong? Are you hurt?". I realized I didn't time that sentence very well. "Yea, I'm fine," I replied. "We need to get answers about something we read in the book. A place we can go to end all this."

Mrs. Cunningham squinted her eyes at me in confusion. She took a glance at Morris and then back at me. "What do you mean you have to talk to Dr. Coleman? You told me he was trying to kill you?" I tried to think of a way to explain but suddenly, Morris interrupts me. "Mrs. Cunningham, I would just listen to him. The last time we ran into this, I was with him. And he was dead on."

Mrs. Cunningham shifted her gaze to Mark, who was still in shock from the explosion. "We can't go to June's now," he said. "They'll be checking with everyone we know after they see you weren't home." Mrs. Cunningham quietly weighed her options and stiffly agreed. I didn't like seeing her look so defeated. But I knew that I probably looked that way too. Mark took an abrupt right turn toward the city hospital.

When we got to the hospital, Morris bolted out of the car. I followed close behind. Mrs. Cunningham yelled something at us into the air, but I couldn't make it out. We ran inside as fast we could. The sound of Mrs. Cunningham's heel echoed behind us. Morris made it to the elevator first. He mashed the UP button over and over as I came up seconds behind him. Mrs. Cunningham was at the front desk talking to the person at the front desk. Her husband was walking in to meet her. The quiet lobby projected their conversation with the front desk.

"Hi, I'm Pamela Cunningham," Mrs. Cunningham said. "We were here last week and left something behind."

"Hello," replied the front desk attendant. "I'm sorry, but the rooms are cleaned regularly. Any items we see are left in the Lost & Found area, which is-"

"No, I understand." Mrs. Cunningham interrupted. "We just wanted to double-check to make sure it wasn't overlooked."

"Ma'am I assure you, there is nothing left in the room you were in."

"Can we just take a quick look? It shouldn't take long."

I took my turn pushing the elevator button. Morris was getting even more anxious. "Can we just take the stairs?" he asked. I didn't even acknowledge his question. Each second standing there made my heart race faster. I didn't know how to control the power I had. I was hoping it would come out when I saw Dr. Coleman again as it did before. I tried not to think about the plan not working as I pushed the elevator button repeatedly.

"What's the last name of the patient?" the attendant asked.

"Foreman," Mrs. Cunningham lied.

A few seconds of empty sound passed by after the faint tapping of the front desk lady's keyboard.

"There doesn't seem to be anything coming up," the attendant said.

I looked back and accidentally made eye contact with the front desk attendant. She looked puzzled for a moment and then looked back at Mrs. Cunningham, who was struggling to get her attention again. The attendant got up from her desk and walked away out of my view. I looked over at Mrs. Cunningham and the worry she felt transferred to me instantly. She looked at her husband.

"Is there a problem, Ms.?" Mark asked. I couldn't hear any reply. Just then, the elevator door opened. Morris and I quickly burst in. The door encased us inside. The escape was a blur so I told Morris to lead the way since I was unconscious when I arrived at the hospital before. Flashes of the doctor's horrifying face started to dampen my determination. My heart started to race at the thought of him being there again.

The soft chimes of the elevator muffled as his words played over and over again, cloaking me in fear. Nausea comforted me with its familiarity. I began to remind myself of how much trouble I was to everyone when the elevator door opened, knocking me out of the trance.

We ran out of the elevator and looked around in a hastened reminiscence. Nurses and doctors flashed their faces at us while braiding their paths from room to room. The attention came and went too much to keep up with. We ran to the room I was in. Before anyone had the chance to say anything about it, we burst in.

An elderly woman, about 70 or 80 years old, laid in the hospital bed covered in a long flowery gown. A blood pressure cuff gripped her left arm with cords that draped down to a small pile on the floor next to her. The laughs from a daytime talk show increase the awkwardness of the situation. The woman didn't seem too distraught by us coming in but was unquestionably confused by us being there. I decided to give Morris a break.

"Hi," I whispered. "We're looking for a doctor that we met in here. We're gonna leave in a second." The woman didn't give the impression that she understood what I was telling her. But I didn't know what else to say. We quickly scanned the room for any signs of Dr. Coleman. Morris checked the bathroom. Nothing. Morris came out of the bathroom with the same result. We sent a gentle wave to the old woman. She was still just staring at us with no words. We left the room and gently closed the door behind us.

I looked around the surrounding rooms. Not wanting to go in, I peered as far as I could through any opening I could see. Dr. Coleman was nowhere in sight. Hopelessness taunted me as we stood stiff in the hospital hallway. I was too ashamed to speak. I thought of the faith Morris had in me earlier in the car and then how things looked after checking the rooms. I made a few more desperate glances through the hall to no avail.

Too much of myself wanted to cry. Tears began to stream down my face faster than I could convince them to stop. I tried to walk away from Morris so he wouldn't notice but the tears blurred my view. I consoled myself the best I had time for, then suddenly, the sound of heavy boots straightened me out. Morris noticed them too. We looked around to pinpoint where the sound was coming from.

Before we were able to find it in time, a tall broad man in an all-black uniform approached us from the hall on the left. His strides were relentlessly focused on getting to us. He pinched the radio near his shoulder. "They're in the Trauma Bay," he said without losing speed. "I found 'em.". I didn't need to hear anything else.

We ran toward the elevators then remembered how long it took to the last time. I darted toward the door with the staircase logo. When I was running, I bumped into Morris who lost his balance and almost fell. I redirected myself and pulled Morris up by the arm. He stumbled back up and kept running. The guard followed our every step.

I shouldered the staircase door open and proceeded to run down. The sound in the staircase swallowed that of the hospital room as the door slammed shut behind us. A few seconds after, the outer sound reemerged as the guard lunges through the door. He was getting closer and closer. I was breathing so hard, my mouth dried up. Pain in my chest tried to convince me to slow down.

Then, I heard Morris yell angrily. I turned around to discover that the guard had grabbed him by the shirt. "No!" I yelled as loud as I could. The sound pulsated into the walls. I turned around but could not catch my footing before tripping and falling down the stairs below me. Everything went dark.

CHAPTER 18

"Mimi ni wa mahali upepo unapoenda. Ndio mahali ambapo makazi yanaishi. Kuwa nami na nitakuwa nawe. Pumzisha roho yako kwenye kifua cha kinga yangu. Kila kitu kitafanikiwa."

//

I jolted up. The cold inside gripped me awake. Cool crisp breezes blew around inside me and demanded my questioning. I felt higher. I looked down and saw that I was above the floor. Levitating.

The look on Morris' face was supposed to frighten me, but there was a surge of many emotions pulsing through me at once. I felt as if I was out of control but also in complete control at the same time.

I recognized I was supposed to be more worried, but I somehow knew I was safe as the emotion I felt belonged as well. Playful fluid washed around in my belly. New but oddly familiar. Before I could focus my thought on the movement, my right arm stiffened out in front of me. Something was flowing through me. Something powerful. My eyes began to well up, slowly glazing a light blueish filter over them. But I didn't lose sight. The world around me became clearer. I put my attention to the guard that was chasing us. But it didn't look like the guard anymore.

The figure that stood behind Morris was disfigured. It had mismatched body parts and a single cracked horn on its head. Its broken teeth were long and yellow. It was seemingly slimy with eyes that were narrow and afraid. Its crookedly-hunched back leaned over Morris. The flow in my hand began to increase in force. I motioned my head for Morris to move. He leaped out of the way onto the floor.

An intense force burst out of my hand. The recoil from the blast nudged me backward a bit, but not much. The blast's waves came and went within seconds, and then the monster flew into the wall of the stairwell. Before I could react, it grit its nasty teeth but only tried to get up for a split second before I sent another pulse blast into it with my left hand. A screech of pain spilled out of it before it disintegrated in front of us. Worry washed over the beast as it realized there was no recovery coming for it. After a few more seconds of pain-induced shrieks, the monster disintegrated, fading from existence.

The world around me seemed to rise as I am lowered back onto my feet from the air. My vision returned to normal, and all I could see is Morris's expression. "Holy bleep, bruh!" Morris screamed. The closed-in area amplified the exclamation. I looked down at my hands, which showed no signs of anything out of the ordinary. I wiggled my fingers to verify that everything was ok. My legs were a bit shaky, but I chalked it up to nerves.

After a few deep breaths, I remembered we could not stay where we were. "We have to go," I mustered. The confidence felt so out of place coming from me. Morris got off of the floor and stood next to me at the bottom of the stairs. His gaze didn't leave me. I assured him that I was ok as much as I could silently. I continued down the stairs as fast as my legs allowed, holding on tightly to the railing. Morris followed close behind, and we eventually made it back to the lobby floor.

Mrs. Cunningham was standing in front of the elevator door. "Mrs. Cunningham!" Morris and I shouted in unison. She quickly turned around and raced toward us. Her husband followed suit from the check-in area.

"We have to get out of here," I said in corroded breaths. The words came out and crumbled apart in front of everyone.

"What's going on?" Mark asked.

"We can explain it in the car. But right now, we have to leave," I replied.

Morris was the first to break the circle. We followed his lead to the lobby's automatic doors. The icy wind blew against us as the hospital's warmed air made way for the intrusion of cold. As soon as we stepped outside, we were met with a big black SUV with armored rims and tinted windows. For a second, we didn't know who it was until we saw the commotion from inside of the passenger side windows. The faint chatter of the communication radios fogged the windows of the vehicle. Mrs. Cunningham grabbed my arm and practically drug me back inside the hospital. Mark and Morris followed her.

The commotion got louder as the doors of the vehicles opened behind us. We ran past the front desk and looked around the lobby for a different exit. Nothing was close by. We headed further into the lobby to find another way. "There! Over there!" Mark shouted. We darted our attention to him. He was pointing to a pathway around the corner in the distance from where we were. We didn't take the time to validate. All of us followed him down the path. The heat from my chest had caught my attention again. The sound in the room had become like objects rushing past my head.

As I reached the corner, a set of double doors could be seen past a security desk. We barged into the automatic doors before they could open for us. The long wall of rooms led to hallways onto the left and right and double doors at the end. We wasted no time rushing to the other side.

Curious eyes peeked through the curtains of a few of the rooms. The sound of our breathing and footsteps echo through the hall, seemingly pulsing off the walls. A few moments passed as we heard the door behind us bust open. The people chasing us were coming full speed. My lungs were filled with heat and grit. The labored breathing from the repeated chases was beginning to represent itself more and more. My legs ached from the constant movement.

I could feel the power of the water that flowed through me help me stay close to the others. Mark occasionally looked back to check the distance between us and the pursuers. The look on his face let me know how close I was to death. We scrunched into each other by the double doors at the end of the long hallway. I took the moment to catch my breath.

Morris looked both ways and sprinted down the left hallway while Mark and Mrs. Cunningham ran down the right one. The people chasing us were almost near us. The look on their faces was focused on me. Their clenched jaws morphed their faces into wolves or rabid dogs. "Braxton! Come on!" shouted Morris from down the hall. I heard his words pass through me, but I felt stuck. Mrs. Cunningham stopped and ran back towards me. Mark followed her. "Run!" Mark yelled at me. I shook myself awake and raced down the hall towards Morris, who had slowed his run down to a jog until we caught up.

A few seconds after, I heard a shriek from Mrs. Cunningham as one of the men rammed her into the double doors at the end of the hallway. I turned around as Mark was falling to the floor from being punched in the face by one of the guards. He tried to get up, but one of the men hit him again and knocked him unconscious.

The double doors slowly closed behind them, swallowing Mrs. Cunningham's scream. Two of the men stepped over Mark and quickly walked towards Morris and I. Suddenly, my stomach began to rumble as I walked backwards down the hall. My hands shook, and I looked for something to grab to keep my balance. I leaned against the wall next to me. I could faintly hear Morris and the other sounds around me slowly muffle as my vision filtered back into the blue haze.

Then, energy started to flow through me like I had just been plugged in. I could feel my posture start to stiffen. My body became sure of itself. I sat up and glared at the men who were approaching us. Their wolf-like faces softened into confusion and concern. My arms pulsed, from my shoulder all the way down to the palms of my hands.

I balled my fist as tightly as I could and lifted it inward in front of me. The guards didn't have time to react before I quickly pulled my fist down and bent their bodies under the heavier gravity. The gurneys and medical carts against the walls crushed like soda cans. Lights in the hall flickered under the pressure. The bodies of the flattened men laid on the floor.

Mrs. Cunningham burst back through the double doors and took a couple of steps toward us before seeing the bodies of men. The look of horror from her seeing Mark unconscious was interrupted as one of the guards re-emerged from the double doors behind Mrs. Cunningham, running into her and tackling her to the ground.

He turned her body over and raised his fist to punch her in the face. I stretched my arm toward him and froze his movements. My arm lifted and the man rose in the air as its true form began to reveal itself in my filtered eyes. I began to shake my hand. Faster than I ever could normally. The body of the man started to shake, matching the movement of my hand as if he was in my grasp.

My hand moved faster and faster until it was like I was in a tremor. Sounds of discomfort spat from the monster as I jolted him around in the air at impossible speeds. It reached for something to grab ahold of, but I made sure there was nothing to help it. Bile began to spew from within the creature all over the hallway walls and floor. I threw its body into the floor, headfirst into its own mess. The sound of its neck cracking rippled through the hallway.

Mrs. Cunningham hastefully drug herself across the floor away from the dead creature, who had started to disintegrate. She looked back at me in panic. Mark rose sluggishly from his attack. His groggy words were inaudible. Mrs. Cunningham quickly crawled to him and held his head in her hands. He blinked himself awake as he sat up. Mark looked around and saw the condensed body of the men. He backed up against the wall.

"It's ok, honey," Mrs. Cunningham whispered. "We're ok." Her shaky voice didn't really seem to believe herself. They both looked up at me. I didn't know how to comfort the look on their faces. I noticed that the blue filter faded back to normal at some point. My body felt a bit tense. I looked down at my palms to see if I noticed any pulsating sensation. Nothing was there.

"We need to go," I heard Morris say from behind me. The stability in his voice resembled mine from earlier. They sat still on the floor in shock for a moment but eventually rose to their feet. I looked back as they moved past me. The scene was intense. Scary. I couldn't help but wonder what I had in me. What I was turning into. I left the bodies behind and followed the group to a hospital exit.

CHAPTER 19

"Death has always intrigued me. One moment, you're here not knowing anything. Holding on to the traditions you were taught. Wandering day after day until something makes you not do so anymore. Eventually, you're dead and you know everything people have always wondered. If there's a God or if it was all made up to help us get through existence. I often wonder if the seconds before death show you your life for a reason. And also, what moments does death show you? What criteria does it use to choose a moment for you to reflect on before it takes you

away? Maybe déjà vu is from us dying a little more every day. Maybe this moment is just a clip I'm watching."

//

My teeth shocked as the frigid wind blew against them. I kept my mouth closed to keep them from hurting. No one was talking so it didn't matter. The silence was louder than bombs after what had happened in the hospital. Mark must have moved the car when Morris and were upstairs because they lead us to a parking garage across the street from the hospital.

Thankfully, the weather softened as we entered. The ripples of our shuffling steps reminded me of the monster that chased us in the stairwell. Its teeth. Its eyes. I knew I would never forget the look on Morris' face. I couldn't help but think about what was going on in his head about what happened. But I decided to let him bring it up when he was ready.

We made it over to where Mark parked the car. Something about being inside it comforted me, even if the comfort was for just a second or two. That seemed to be the same for the others as everyone took a deep breath at the same time. "Where are we going?" Mrs. Cunningham asked. Her voice was foreign in the silence. No one answered right away. After a moment, Mark helped with the dangling question.

"What about the cabin?" Mark asked. "We could stay there, at least until we know what's going on."

"That could work. What do we do about the parents though?" Mrs. Cunningham replied. "We can't just take their kids."

"This seems to be a different kind of situation. It's for their safety."

"I *know*. But, we still need to tell them what's going-"

Morris stepped in. "I can text my dad to let him know I'll be late getting home." Silence returned. I didn't know what to say so I blurted out what came to mind. "You don't have to tell my mom anything. It probably doesn't matter to her anyway." The sentence didn't let me filter it. That time, the silence was because of me. The quiet was thicker than before. Hotter. I looked out of the window to search for something else to think about. I decided to focus on the fog my breath was making on the glass. The start of the engine let me know that they were not going to put up a fight.

Mark fidgeted with the radio for a little while and eventually stopped on a station that sounded like old cartoons. Morris and Mrs. Cunningham scrolled around on their phones. After a few minutes, I noticed my eyes starting to get heavy. The washing around in my stomach mellowed itself still. I fought the incoming sleep closing in on me. I thought about anything that would keep me up. I had run more than I ever have before in my life and my body noticed. Drifting in and out of alertness was frustrating. I contemplated giving in to slumber but felt it was unfair to rest.

I heard the conversation from Mark and Mrs. Cunningham dodging in between lyrics on the radio. Mumblings of where we were going to go. What I did at the hospital. *How* I did what I did at the hospital. Mrs. Cunningham still seemed to be in some kind of shock. Which made me question how calm I was. I didn't like being talked about like I was already dead. I hesitated at first but couldn't pretend not to hear them any longer.

"I didn't ask for this," I spat before I could think of anything proper to say. Mrs. Cunningham looked back at me from the passenger seat. I didn't know what the look on my face would seem like, so I turned away. "I don't know what's going on." Heat started to rise from my neck to my face. Mrs. Cunningham placed her hand on mine, which was all that was needed to break my walls down. Tears started to stream from my face. "I thought this was *done*!" I yelled through the hurt. "We did *everything*!"

Mrs. Cunningham started a reply, but the impact from the collision took her breath away. A black SUV had rammed into the back of Mark's car, nearly swiveling us off the road. I looked back and see the tinted eyes of Ms. Lee in the passenger seat. Her demonic gaze met my eyes with a mix between anger and excitement.

"Damn it!" Mrs. Cunningham shouted. "It's Barbara!" Mark tried to make out the face in the rearview mirror but the rattle from the 2nd hit blurred the reflection. That time, the car fishtailed for a while before Mark was able to gain control again. "Sit back!" he shouted in a panic. Mark sped up through the traffic around us. Honking cars and angry faces rushed out of view next to us as we weaved through the snowy streets.

Morris backhanded me softly in the chest. "You good?" he asked unsteadily. I self-assessed and realized he was talking about my breathing. I sat still for a moment to collect the air around me. As my thoughts slowed down, I tried to figure out what to do. I quickly brought my attention to the men at the hospital.

I closed my eyes and checked for anything, anything at all, that felt the same. Nothing. I pounded my belly where the water I felt before resided to get it to come up. I only felt a twinge from me hitting myself. Mark whipped around a mail truck to keep from hitting it. We swayed sharply to the right, then to the left, and finally back centered again as he continued down the street. Faint honking faded in the background.

The SUV pulled up to the side of us. Ms. Lee's slimy grin saw the fear on my face. She mouthed something I couldn't make out. Mark slammed on his brakes sharply and took a hard right down a crossroad. The SUV didn't seem to have caught on yet. The voices around me blanketed over themselves as everyone in the car shouted at each other about the attack. Heat and chills traded places within me trying to discover how to feel.

I was shaken back to life by Morris who seemed to have been trying to get my attention for more than he wanted to. "What are we going to do?" He asked. His eyes were wide with fright and confusion. I didn't have an answer to offer. Only a look that didn't satisfy his inquiry. My headache was rising. There wasn't any help I could give so I cradled my head in my hands.

Then, the crying of tires caught my attention. I looked up and saw the SUV charging towards us again from the left. "Go!" I yelled, almost too late. Mark managed to speed up the car just enough for the large SUV to barely miss us. Morris and I checked the back window for a crash but there wasn't one. The SUV whipped around like a tail of a snake and continued towards.

Ms. Lee screamed something into a cell phone and threw it aggressively into the street. Remnants of the device flew into the air but disappeared after only a couple of seconds behind their vehicle. They were charging towards us so fast, it looked like we were going backward. I clinched the headrest of the backseat. "Mark, go!" Mrs. Cunningham yelled at the top of her lungs. They were racing towards us faster and faster. I braced for an inevitable impact, turning away right when the SUV was about to hit us again at full speed.

But it didn't. Instead, they swerved over to the left of us again. But that time, Ms. Lee had her door opened and was preparing to jump into Mark's car. "Oh my God." Mrs. Cunningham said softly, watching Ms. Lee steady herself. "She's gonna jump. Mark! She's going to jump!" shouted Mrs. Cunningham.

Ms. Lee leaped out of the SUV and onto the rear side of Mark's vehicle. An assortment of shrieks and hollers filled the car. Morris grabbed onto my coat and pulled me away from the monster. The long claws of Ms. Lee sunk into the body of the car like a nail through an aluminum can. The sound of peeling metal sent chills through my body.

"Hang on!' Mark yelled. He jerked the car side to side to shake Ms. Lee off. She groaned at the movement but didn't lose her grip. Mrs. Cunningham looked back in horror as her colleague continued to cling to the car. "I can't get her off!" Mark blurted. Then, Ms. Lee started punching the window. Her punches were unnaturally fast. The cracks spread wider and longer with each hit. I kicked the door to try to knock her off, but she wouldn't budge. My fear seemed to fill her with joy. The faint cackling sound from her throat felt like one of pleasure.

Without warning, Mrs. Cunningham grabbed the sterling wheel and smashed us into the SUV next to us. Ms. Lee. shrieked at impact. Mark instantly caught on and did it again. Mark swerved as he noticed the oncoming traffic on the other side of the street. He rammed the side of the car into the SUV one final time. But he didn't let off. He pressed up against the SUV and forced it into the oncoming traffic. The crash sounded like an explosion next to us. A couple of cars slid into the SUV's large black frame. The small pile-up became smaller in the back window as we continued down the road.

Ms. Lee was worn down some from having her body smashed over and over again but did not give up on her pursuit. "You shall perish, Boy of Midland!" she yelled through the window. Mark drifted into the other side of the street. "What are you doing?" Mrs. Cunningham gripped onto Mark's arm. "I'm getting rid of her," He replied through gritted teeth.

Mark got as close as he could to the edge of the road. Mark sped up and banged Ms. Lee's body against the signs, mail drop-offs, and bus stop benches that lined the city streets. She whimpered as each object blasted against her. Bent signs and broken benches fell behind us. Mark honked through the oncoming traffic approached us. Angry faces smeared the windows as we raced by them.

Then Ms. Lee banged her narrow head against the window, never separating her eyes from me. The splattered blood streaked the cracked glass. She grinned at the look of shock I had on my face. Suddenly, she rushed downward, out of my view. She was scary when she was there, but I was even more scared when I couldn't see her. I looked around the car for her but couldn't find her. There was no sign that she fell off.

I peered out my window again. Before I had time to act, Ms. Lee bit into the rear passenger side tire. The car dropped down to the rim and scrapped the snowy street. Ms. Lee leaped backward off the car and onto the sidewalk, a piece of the tire still in her mouth. Mark couldn't gain control of the vehicle. The car almost hit two pedestrians as we grinded down the street. The screeching was as if the car itself was screaming. We were headed into the rear of a parked car when the garbage truck rammed into us at full speed.

The car spun around and turned numerous times until we landed upright at the guardrail of the street above the nearby lake. Everything seemed to have been in slow motion until we stopped. My headache was now full and thorough. I slowly unbuckled my seatbelt and fell out of the mangled car. The frozen gravel wasn't concerned for me as its cold spread onto my arms like poisonous vines. A familiar dizziness began to rise inside me. My legs were shaking violently. I grab onto the frigid car and pulled myself up.

Morris was already on his way out. I wanted to say something, but the words wouldn't start.

Morris didn't seem to be able to say much either. The road was littered with filthy snow and car parts. All traffic dissipated from the area. I started to find standing to be too much. I went over to Mrs. Cunningham's door near me on the passenger side of the car to get her out. When I opened the door, Mrs. Cunningham spilled from the car onto the cold street.

She laid there still with blood dripping down her head into her open eyes. "Pam?" I heard from inside the car. Mark had just become conscious and seen Mrs. Cunningham collapsed in the street. "Pamela!" he shouted thought a cracked voice as he unbuckled his seatbelt and stumbled out of the car. The panic in his groans grew in his voice the closer he got to us.

Mark's labored breathing and whimpering lifted the horror in my heart. I stared at her, hoping she would start coughing and get up like I had seen in the movies. But it became clearer and clearer with each fleeting second that I was staring at an empty body. Morris gripped his head with both hands at the sight of her. "No, no, no, no, no," he murmured to himself.

Suddenly, the light of the sun blinked, dimming our view for a split second. Its slight warmth left and returned. I looked up and saw the trailer of a semi-truck hurdling towards us from down the street. Ms. Lee's driver stood in the far distance in the middle of the road. Right when Mark was about to reach his wife and the fast-approaching vehicle was about to smash us, the ground gave way.

We sank into the street like falling through thin ice. I tried to reach up for something but there was nothing to grab. My stomach felt as if I was starting a big drop on a roller coaster. My scream was muffled into silence by the dark we had collapsed into. Before I had time to panic, we reemerged onto a surface again. But we weren't on the street from before. We were in a cave.

The air was different and hard to adjust to at first. Mark looked around for Mrs. Cunningham's body, but she was nowhere to be found. Morris fell to his knees beside me. The room full of scattered crackled pillars of rock was like the one from the book. "The entry was an exit," I murmured. "The exit of a life." Mark's shouts for his wife rose and faded, soaking into to space around us. "Wha-what happened, Braxton?" Morris asked, seemingly scared and finally fully broken. I glanced at him and looked away in shame. "We're in the Pit of War," I replied.

CHAPTER 20

"Being lost is not only a location but also a state of mind. We typically don't fully know where things are going to go in our life. Who is to say we aren't all always lost? Why do we only mention wandering when we are on our feet? Our minds wander constantly. Maybe we are lost in the days we live. Some may have a better sense of direction of what to do when it comes to their days, but there isn't anyone on Earth that knows where they are guaranteed to go."

//

The heat of tears rolled down my face as we sat separated in the dusty cave. Mark's breathing got faster and harder until the room was filled with only his sound. Morris attempted a small effort to help, but there was nothing he was able to do. Mark rocked back and forth on the floor of the cave rubbing his wedding ring. I tried to focus on the dancing ache in my head to shoo away the despair. The cave's stench reminded me of the old library underneath the record store. I took out the book from my backpack for answers to what to do.

"I'm going to look up what to do to get us out of here," I managed to crackle out of my dry throat. Mark and Morris didn't seem interested. Them ignoring me reminded me of who I was. It was dumb of me to try. I wiped the tears away and started reading some of what the book said. Then a shadow stood over me, blocking the light.

"What do you got?" Morris asked. His tone was manufactured and defeated. I tried to make it worth his efforts. "I'm just looking for anything more about this place. Seeing what we have to do to get out of here and end this," I replied. Morris sat next to me on the ground of the cave. He stared at the pages, searching with me for any answers we could find.

"Look at this right here," I said, pointing to one of the pages. I leaned the page over in Morris' direction. He looked confused. "You can read that?" he asked. I looked at the page again, and then back at Morris. "I'm talking about this right here," I say, pointing again at the text on the page. Morris took another glance. He squinted his eyes at me and leaned back. He was starting to worry me.

"Yo, Mark," Morris shouted out, keeping his eyes on me. "Come here, real quick." Mark gathered the needed strength and made his way over to us. "Yea," he said, coldly. "My phone broke in the crash so I can't translate any of this, but Braxton told me he can read this," Morris said, nudging his head towards the book. Mark kneeled and checked over the page we were talking about. After a few seconds, he stuck his neck out to get a closer look. "What do you mean you can read this?" Mark asked.

I couldn't quite understand how I was able to read the book. But I could. Over time, I had felt like I had gotten closer to the book. I started to understand it more. It was becoming a part of me. I looked down at the words on the page. I knew exactly what they said. I tried to wrap my head around what was happening, but things were odd enough. At that point, anything could have happened, and it would be hard to question.

Mark and Morris backed up away from me. "This is crazy!" Mark hollered in the air. I looked down at the book that I held in my arms. The tree-like cover and aged yellowing pages made me think it had a story of its own to tell. I lowered my head, feeling as if I had to speak for the poor book that couldn't speak for itself. The horrors it must have seen over the years. The voiceless assistance it tried to give, only to be taken and shoved behind a shelf of other books. I brought the book closer to my chest, finally realizing that I was actually embracing myself.

I forgot anyone else was there after a few moments. After some time passed, I opened the book again to continue the search for answers. Mark sat with us momentarily. I explained each page like a teacher to their students. More and more mysteries started to unfold. Morris asked a lot of the questions as Mark looked on in silence. I explained to him what the book mentioned about the room to see if he could help us understand it. I tried to be as cautious as possible when explaining how I thought we got in the cave. The time felt like it rushed past us as we were about a quarter of the way through it.

I read the words aloud the best I could. A lot of the information didn't make any sense. I tried to absorb as much as I could. The information seemed to soak into me the more I read. Mark paced the area from time to time, still silent. Neither of us pressed him. Each time I looked at him, it reminded me of Mrs. Cunningham. Flashes of her lifeless body intruded on my focus. Her bloody face and dead eyes were something I would never forget. I felt ashamed to dismiss the thoughts, but keeping them in my mind burned from the inside.

Page after page of the book taught me phrases to think about in order to better control my abilities. Meditations and inner chants seemed to be really important. The book said it is more important to think the words in your mind than to say them out loud. Morris was seemingly losing interest, but I kept looking for anything that could help us. Suddenly, Mark rushes towards us.

"Alright look, man," he stated, "I don't know what's going on here, but you need to do something because I'm not going to stay here the rest of my life! You did something to get us here with… those powers or whatever, so you can do it again to get us out"

The expression on his face was filled with worry and anger. His clenched fist put me on guard. My thoughts seized and awaited release.

"I'm trying, but I can't find anything," I replied.

"Well look harder!"

"Do you think I want to be down here?"

"I just want to get out here and back – back to Pamela."

The thought of Mrs. Cunningham softened the atmosphere. I didn't respond, fearful that the off chance of a comment may sound like I'm undermining her death. Mark's sniffles started my heart. The tears returned. And I let them. She deserved them. Images of her talking to me after class flash through my mind. Her smile. Her concern.

Knowing that I was the reason Mrs. Cunningham had died sent me to a place of anguish that I had never felt before. My chest ached more as the memories replayed. I already missed her so much. I knew that if she was there, she would have something to say to make all of us smile. She was that kind of person. Sitting there at that moment, we began to understand what would happen in a world without her.

Mark slowly turned around. "I'm going to find a way out of here," he said wiping his face. I thought about stopping him, but I didn't know how to. He made his way into the dim abyss ahead. Morris sat in silence on the floor of the cave. My body was worn and was still sore from the crash. I hadn't moved much since I'd been down in the Pit of War. The shock of it all was started to fade. I noticed a sharp pain on my side when I tried to reposition. But I knew I couldn't focus on what was wrong. I had to make things right.

The pages of the book patiently waited for me as I looked back through what I had read. I got familiar with the odd pictures and symbols. I was drawn back to the pages about meditation. I had always heard of meditation but have never done it. The words on the page seemed like water to my soul. The more I read, the more I wanted to read. I did not realize how interested I would be in it.

I rubbed my fingers over the words on the rough paper. I repeated the words over and over again until I could say them without looking. I closed my eyes as the water in my belly started to build into a tide. My whole body became cool. The flow within me started to spread all around, almost dancing. It swayed me. The faint sounds of the cave slowly washed away into a calm silence. The feeling was one I felt as if I was supposed to have all along. Untroubled bliss.

"Boy of Midland," the voice in front of me said. My eyes burst open as the unfamiliar voice startled me. She was a beautiful young girl with glistening milk chocolate skin. Markings on her face looked like some of the pictures in the book. The blossomed headscarf only partially covered her oversized hoop earrings. Her eyes were sharp but soft and welcoming. The confidence they were filled with immediately made me disregard her petite stature.

The air around her shimmered and followed her movements as she motioned for me to come closer. The glowing purple and blue shawl draped over her long blue dress seemed to flow with her. Her fingers were garnished with rings of gold and tattoos that glowed in the shadowy room. "Come. You will not be harmed," she said softly to me when she noticed my hesitation.

A warm peace washed over me, letting me know everything was safe. I slowly walked toward the young girl. Her gentle smile complimented her elegance. "I've been waiting to finally meet you," she said. Her kindness reminded me of Mrs. Cunningham. The girl seemed to have felt my thoughts.

"I am truly sorry," she said, gently.

"It's – it's fine," I lied.

"You are such a strong boy, Braxton."

I hesitated. "Strong" wasn't how I would have defined myself. The young girl placed her hand on my shoulder. "You are a *strong* boy, Braxton." I smiled softly and nodded my head in thanks. I shook myself out of my negative thoughts.

"Who are you?" I questioned.

"I am from a time ago," the young girl replied. "We should only speak of what is truly important."

Her unwavering look awaited another question from me. Although nothing made sense, I struggled to find anything to say. I rummaged through my thoughts and blurted the first thing that came to mind. "Can you bring Mrs. Cunnin-" The words caught in my throat before I could finish saying them. They burned coming out. It was hard having to ask. Glimpses of Mrs. Cunningham's bloody face framed in the center of my mind.

"Can you bring Mrs. Cunningham back?" Tears welled up in my eyes as I managed to get the sentence out, slowly covering the girl and revealing her again as they ran down my cheeks. The young girl gently placed her hand on my face. Her touch was warm and electric. Her pleasant scent was like something I had never smelled before.

The girl wiped my tears away with her thumb. She took a moment to cradle my head in her hands. She looked into my eyes in a way that no one ever had before. The look of care and concern on her face almost made my pain worse but I managed to contain myself. She didn't have to give me an answer. I understood.

"What are those things chasing me?" I asked after a few seconds of silence. The girl did not answer. Instead, she continued to look at me. Her eyes were softened a bit but still very intentional. "What about that record store? What was that?" She remained silent. I paused to think hard about what was important. What was *truly* important. I sifted through my curiosities, searching for what mattered. Then it hit me.

"What did I do wrong?" I blurted. "Why is this still happening after I did everything I was supposed to?"

"You are the only one that could, Braxton." The girl replied. "This is meant for you."

"What do you mean? Why me?"

"You are different than others. You bit the fruit of our people. But it was meant to be."

My mind went back to what Nikki told me about that horrible day. I thought about how hard it was for her to tell me. The pain I saw as she wept for me. For my soul.

"So, am I going to die?" I asked.

The girl fell silent again.

"Ok, uh," I struggled to regain her access. "Why is me biting the fruit so important?"

"You obtained the power that was meant for The Profligate."

I pondered a moment before realizing who she was referring to. "Do you mean that 'Stellan' person?" I asked.

The girl shrieked. She clenched her chest and doubled over. My heart seized with sharp whining pain. The blackened world we were in pulsed red, permeating my peripheral vision. The hissing in my ear was deafening. My eyes forced themselves shut and my stomach began to bubble with protest. Gradually, the siren of anguish started to subside. As the grip of pain loosened, I began to breathe again.

I rose up light-headed and was met with the enraged eyes of the young girl. Her still and motionless gaze scared me inside and out. She was hunched over and pointing directly at me. Goosebumps covered my whole body. I was petrified. Her eyes shifted into a more narrow position. Her gritted teeth pried open, but only slightly. "Do not *ever* say that name aloud again!" she ordered. Her bark was louder than her expression acknowledged, but it was real. And I felt it.

She did not grant time for a response. She took a moment, blinking away the oncoming tears in her eyes. She stood straight up as before, wiped her nose, and untucked her tongue from the inner corners of her mouth. After a hard, sharp, breathy exhale, she returned her gaze to one of awaiting a question. Her eyes were only slightly watery but were as stable as they were previously.

"I need to know how to get us out of here. How do we end this and go home?" I asked.

"Rectification will ensue," she replied. "All will be as is destined."

"So how do we do it? Where is the way out?"

The girl's eyes shifted downward. Just before I began to question what was going on, her eyes returned to me.

"The final sands are nearing the bottom of our hourglass, Boy of Midland," she replied. "She is on her way."

She drew a small square in front of her with her index finger. With a soft blow, the square pushed forward, expanding in size. The sound of gentle water rushed past as the now large square rested behind me. Lights around the trim of the square brightened the world around us. "What do you mean?" I asked. "So that's it? You can't tell me anything else?" The girl's silence answered me.

I tried to think of something else to say but nothing came to fruition. The moment became panicked. I gave one final look at the girl, who remained motionless. I turned toward the square-shaped portal. I examined it briefly before slowly putting my hand through its opening. There was no feeling. No pain or sensation. No change in temperature. Nothing. I took a step inside.

"Braxton," The girl called quietly.

I turned around at the sound of my name. She sounded muffled but still audible. The look on her face was somber.

"He *has* to," She murmured.

"Wha-," My reply was lost as she gently closed her open hand into a fist and sealed the portal.

CHAPTER 21

"I never know when I'm making the right decision. No one ever does. How could you? We take past experiences and assume life is going to be exactly how it was before. I don't know exactly how or for what, but life has a very clever way of figuring out what you're thinking and making sure that you end up the most hurt and confused that you possibly can. It's almost as if life is protective of itself. Like we are intruding on its existence. We take it and call it 'our life' when in actuality, it was never ours to possess. We claim to give life when we aren't able to even

govern our own. When a person 'loses' a life, they actually had never found it in the first place. We are here on borrowed breaths hoping we made the right decisions when we have to put our empty bodies back on the shelf in our boxes."

//

My body naturally gasped for air as I came back. I patted myself while I caught my breath, examining my clothes to see if they were wet. They weren't. The book sat patiently in my hands like it did when I left. Morris was asleep to my left. I had no clue how long I'd been gone. The dingy aroma of the cave returned to me like the smell of a bad dream. Mark was still nowhere in sight. I tried to tune out Morris' snoring to see if I heard him lurking around nearby. Nothing. I took a deep breath and leaned my head back against the wall of the cave to process what had happened.

Suddenly, a heavy boom jolted me up from the floor of the cave. Scattered shrieks and hollering could be heard in the far distance. The sound gradually got a bit louder as I stood there. Something sounded like it was banging against the walls. It hit over and over again, echoing through the cave. The inconsistent pillar-like beams helped the noise travel to us. Before I could react, Morris was standing next to me, now fully awake. "What was that?" he asked through a scratchy throat. I couldn't think of what to say. But then, I was finally able to make out a voice in the midst of all the racket.

"Where do thou hide, Boy of Midland?"

Chills ran all over my body. Morris grabbed my sleeve tightly. "That's you! That's what they call you, right?" He asked, looking at me intensely. I nodded. Echoes of the shuffling ahead redirected our attention. "Disperse!" yelled a distance growl. "Spill every drop of blood from the child and bring me his damned pate!" The deafening cheers rang through the catacombs. "Hail Stellan!" shouted the voices. The crowd repeated the words with enthusiasm and vigor. The shouts sounded like there could be hundreds of them. "We have to get out of here," I whispered.

Morris looked around for a moment. There didn't seem to be many places to run to.

"Where's Mark?" Morris asked.

"I don't know," I replied. "He never came back. We have to find him."

"No, we *don't*. That's a grown man."

"We can't just leave him!"

"*He* left *us*, didn't he?"

"He was trying to find a way out!"

"Well, his way out is death now!"

The sound in the room felt smaller as the scattered footsteps seemed to surround us more with every moment. Bits of laughter and growling and banging rippled between the irregular pillar-like fixtures, becoming empty air as it approached us. "Quick, this way," I hissed, heading to the left. Morris grabbed my sleeve again. "Wait…" I stopped and looked at him.

"Let's split up," Morris mutterd in a hushed voice.

"What? Again? Why?" I countered.

"Because you got that water junk. If they get you and the book too, it's over!"

"This thing's gonna start hollering if you touch it."

"Just keep it in the bag! It probably won't be able to tell who has it."

"Well, I don't wanna find out by it screaming and getting us killed!"

"Just giv-"

A loud boom in the distance to the far right interrupted us. We ran through a web of empty areas until the sound felt like it was further away. The flames in the torches swayed as we ran past them. I labored my breathing to catch my breath more quietly. Morris peeked through the dimly lit openings to make sure we were in the clear. "What was that?" Morris asked once he thought it was safe. I shrugged my shoulders and shook my head, still trying to regain composure from the abrupt running. I had hoped it wasn't Mark, but there was no way of telling. My heart was beating so fast, it was difficult to think straight. The echoes around us seemed to be getting louder. More frequent. The heat of fear covered my entire body.

"We can't stay here," I said to Morris.

"I know," he replied. "But where are we gonna go?"

I poked my ear out of the hole next to us, searching for sounds to run from. The left was quieter, although I could still hear some of them. "We have to try this way," I commanded, pointing my thumb to the exit. With no objection, Morris followed me into the dim path forward.

The ashy ground made it hard to be quiet. Each step seemed to travel through the whole cave. I tried to mimic my steps like my days in the Streetrat Bootcamp with Nikki to make our my quieter when another boom went off. Morris and I ducked at the impact. Right after, I heard yelling and what sounded like a faster movement than before. "Maybe that's Mark!" I exclaimed. I started to head toward the sound when suddenly, Morris grabbed me by the arm.

"Bruh, wait," Morris whispered.

"For what?" I replied. The words spat out of me in confusion and anger.

"We can't run up on these things! We don't even know if it's him or not."

"We can't just hide here and find out later, either! He could be hurt!"

"Ok. Ok, I got a plan," Morris said, looking toward the blast.

"We're not splitting up, Morris."

"Why not?" Morris snapped.

The yelling in the distance got louder and rowdier. It had become harder to make out where it was as the echoes seemed to be all around us. Panic began to rise in me. "We can't stand here," Morris warned, running towards one of the rooms in front of us. I followed him in, hoping he knew where he was going. The screeching and howling made the idea of getting caught unbearable. Images of being beaten and torn apart little by little while they enjoyed themselves flashed in my mind. I had no clue how if I could fight them all. Or what they truly wanted from me. I just knew I had it and couldn't let them get it.

"Ok," I said hesitantly. I took the bag off my shoulder and extended it towards Morris.

"Are you sure?" He asked, just as hesitant.

"You're faster than me. Even if they see you, you have a better chance of getting away than I do. And you're right. If they kill me, they at least won't have me *and* the book."

Morris reached out to grab the bag until suddenly we heard my name. "Braxton! Run!" It was the sound of someone terrified. Someone running. It was Mark. In and out of the barely lit web of pillars in the catacombs, I could make out Mark racing towards us waving his hand in front of him. Go!" he called out at the top of his lungs. Not very far behind him was a stampede of odd beings with torches. Some with dog-like features. Some with those of men.

I stood frozen until Morris grabbed me by the shirt and pulled me out of the room. I threw the bag back over my shoulder and ran through the cave. Loud snarling rang through my ear, seemingly getting closer and closer. Pops and bangs could be heard around us. Clanking scrapes of metal pulsed through the atmosphere. Each room looked the same. It was hard to tell if we were running in circles or not. And there was no time to make sure.

When things got distant enough, I stopped to breathe. Sweat rained down my face into my eyes. The burning stung, so I squeezed my eyes shut. I was too scared to move. The noises of the things chasing us came in and out. I checked the room for another set of breaths. I couldn't hear any. I took another moment to check but I couldn't hear anything through the hollering around me.

"Morris," I murmured. I slowly peeked around the cavity of the room, looking for any movement. I couldn't see any. "Morris!" My whisper got harsher and raspier. Still no reply. Thick heat washed over me. I checked around the corner for shadows. When it seemed safe, I crept out of the room, looking for any sign of Morris. I cautiously called out his name one more time and stuck my ear into the shadowy rooms for any answer.

My breathing started to pick up as my worry grew more with each passing second. The openness of the maze of rooms made me think I didn't have much time to stand still. Something could make its way around into where I was. I kept moving, peeking around the openings I came across.

My search got louder and more desperate. Ideas of running through the cave came to mind. I tried to focus and make my powers start, but they wouldn't come. I repeated the words I remembered from the book to get back to the young girl I met. I said them over and over, hoping she would appear and help us with any of this. Nothing happened.

Frustration rose within me. Tapes of my mom telling me I was just a stooge, and I could never be a person that could do anything right replayed in my mind as it had many times before. My thoughts spiraled teachers telling me that I wouldn't be good at much because I was fat and needed to get disciplined to be worth anything. I started to recall kids at school smiling and shaking their heads while they gazed at me every time I came out of my comfort zone to get their approval. I began to recognize that all the things that were happening weren't just a string of bad luck. I caused harm to everything I existed around.

Nearby shuffling postponed my oncoming tears. I stood still to hear where the sound was coming from. It was quick bursts of movement that started and stopped sporadically. I leaned closer to the noise, keeping my guard up just in case. That's when I noticed the long dark jacket sleeve with the Midland Viking logo on it. Morris.

I looked left and right, to make sure nothing was there, and then tip-toed closer. Almost too slow. I didn't know if it was safe to call out yet, so I tried to get to him before he moved again. But each time I felt I was close, Morris ran behind one of the other pillars. I moved faster, fashioning my steps into silent paces. Distant growling rumbled through the air, redistributing my attention to the other side of me.

After a few moments, I tried again more quickly. I wanted so bad to blurt his name or throw something to get his attention. But I knew that would jeopardize us both. I stood at one of the openings and waited for him to move again. When he darted from pillar to pillar, I waved frantically, hoping he would notice me. He didn't.

I continued my path following him between the gap of rooms. I weaved into one a little closer. When the time was right, I waved again, but with both hands above my head. He missed it again. Looking around once more, I made another quick dash between rooms, closing our gap even further. Finally, Morris saw me moving.

He stopped for a second to see if it was me. I leaned out from behind the pillar, quickly waving. He nodded when he realized I made it. We both checked to see if the coast was clear. "Where are they?" he mouthed from afar. All the times we were reading each other's lips in class was finally helping us. "I don't know," I mouthed back, shaking my head. I briefly looked over the surrounding area. The clatter seemed somewhat close but not in our immediate vicinity.

I paced through a couple of rooms over to him. "Where did they go?" Morris asked as he was approaching me. I started to reply when the grinning head of one of the beings quickly peeked around the pillar behind Morris. The look of shock on my face surprised Morris, making him turn around. The demon's smile turned into lust and hunger as it rushed from behind the pillar and charged towards us.

Morris froze as the being reached out to grab him. Before I could think about reacting, my eyes quickly tinted to the familiar soft blue color. The water within me awakened and energy pulsated through me. I stuck my arm out toward the being. Morris dived behind me as the energy blast burst out of my hand and onto the demon's body. It flew back, plunging into the pillar at the end of the room, and slowly disintegrated away.

My eyes were beginning to turn to normal as the pillar the demon landed into loudly cracked in half. I only had time to turn around before the rock ceiling above use came down, piling on top of my lower half. My head banged against the hard cave floor. Underneath the side of my head became wet with my blood. I tried to speak but nothing came out. My vision faded in and out of blindness.

Morris quickly came running up to me. He crawled over on his hands and knees, lowering himself down to look into my eyes. "Braxton? Braxton?" I heard him call out. His voice was faint and muffled in my ears. I gathered as much strength as I could and reached my hand toward him to pull me out. But he didn't. Morris stood up. Then he pulled the bag off of my back and put it over his shoulder. I tried to look up but couldn't raise my head high enough to see more than him running away.

CHAPTER 22

Running. Running fast. Through a hall. School. Upstairs. Panicked. Faster. Helping Braxton. They're chasing me. Even faster. Tired. Worried. Confused. Someone's grabbing me. Evil eyes. Hate. Evil eyes. Whispers. Anger. Betrayal. Evil smile. Survival. I see Braxton. Mrs. Cunningham. Worried. Book. Get book. Sad. Dark. Dark. Dark.

//

The hurtful images repeatedly faded into the bleak darkness of the cave. It felt hotter than before. My legs lay pinned down under the weighty debris. My head was pounding. It was hard to fully open my eyes. Hard to breathe. Scrapes and thuds pulsed in and out of my hearing behind me. Sounds that were not my own.

I tried to turn to see what it could be but only managed to get my head halfway. Out of the corner of my eye, I saw a figure coming in and out. They were moving quickly. Unorganized. The thuds matched the movement of the thing coming towards me. A gasp of sound escaped from within me. They stopped. Quick footsteps made their way to me. "-ton?" I heard. I tried to raise myself but could barely move. Every movement demanded strength from me that I no longer had. "I'm gonna get you out of here," the figure encouraged, running back behind me. After a few more grunts, the thuds stopped, and they came back to me.

My arms lifted unexpectedly, and I felt a tug. First lightly, then harder. My sore legs became lighter as the rubble fell away. I had a hard time standing up straight. Mark reached his arm up under me for support. "Ok, hold on. Hold on," he said, trying to keep me upright. My head was pounding. The dizziness almost knocked me back to the ground. The ache squinted my eyes. I took a second to catch my breath. The spinning of the room eventually slowed to only a slight spiral. I tested my legs to make sure I could walk. Mark's hand hovered over my back as I hobbled around the corner of the room. The absent weight of my bag rushed me into hot anger. But also, sadness. And confusion. Morris was one of them. Even the thought felt out of place.

"We have to find Morris," I said, bitterly.

"Where is he?" Mark replied.

"I don't know. But he has the book."

Mark glanced at my back, remembering the bag that had been with me. His face showed me he was putting the pieces back together.

"Do you mean he-" Mark started.

"Yea," I interrupted. "The whole time."

Disbelief's silence rose. It was hard to verbalize anything. Mark recognized that I didn't want to speak. "I was wondering what happened," he said. He continued with the puzzle of events. "When I was running, it got quiet. Almost as if they turned around and gave up. But I knew that didn't happen. I hid until I knew it was safe to look around. Then I heard a huge explosion or something."

He pointed at the pile of rubble that had collapsed on me. It was hard to believe I was under all the mess there. I knew the power within me protected me from having broken legs. Or worse. "I blasted one of those demon things," I murmured. "It hit that pillar and it came down on me. Morris took the bag and left." I rushed the words out, trying to get the sentence over with. The sadness burned. I could feel the collar of my shirt heating up. Embarrassment flushed my whole body. I was embarrassed of being so sad. Embarrassed of caring so much. Embarrassed of allowing myself to believe someone could be a real friend of mine.

Mark shook me out of my trance. I couldn't accept his concern. I took his hand off my shoulder and lightly limped past him into one of the room's openings. "We need to get going if we're going to find him," I directed. A weak attempt to redirect the attention. Mark seemed to agree as he followed me down that passage through the cave.

It was quieter. Much quieter than before. We seemed to be the only ones in the whole cave. Wondering if Morris knew a way out the whole time only brought up more anger. I tried to put my mind somewhere else but there was nowhere else for it to go. Mark and I peeked through room after room for anything that looked different. The catacombs seemed to go on forever.

Then, we heard something. "Shh. Shh," Mark ordered, holding out his hand for me to stop. We paused to hone in our hearing of the sound. Muffled banter from a distance hummed through the air. I couldn't hear what they were saying. Mark didn't seem to get much from it, either. Suddenly the scattering got closer and closer. Pulses of heat washed over me.

Just then, the familiar sound of rumbling picked up in the distance. The sound of the demons reemerged. I reached for my bag before remembering it was gone. "They're coming!" Mark blurted once he realized what was happening. "Can't you do something?" he pleaded. I stood in shock at the thought that Morris had told them where we were. My heart dropped to my stomach. Morris was sending them to finish me. After a couple of muffled seconds, I realized Mark was yelling at me to run.

We ran as fast as we could deeper into the cave and hid behind two separate pillars not too far from each other. Panic set in more and more as we stood there waiting to get killed. The confusion of everything that was happening got heavier to hold. My body ached slow but constant. I leaned my head back against the pillar and the tears finally freed themselves. Slow whimpered heaves bellowed from within me. It became uncontrollable. Too scared to move, I let the tears tickle my face until they began to dry on their own.

"Braxton!" I peered to my left where I see Mark trying to get my attention. He nudged his head for me to come closer to him. The distance wasn't much but felt like miles at the moment. I carefully peered down the hazy dimness of the cave in front of me, then behind. Nothing was in sight. I peeled off the pillar to creep over to Mark when a voice stopped me in my tracks.

"Mark! Mark, help me!" The distant cry jolted my heart. "Pam?" responded Mark in a trembling voice. "Mark! Please!" Mark burst into a sprint towards the voice of Mrs. Cunningham in the distance. My heart raced at the sound of her screams. Worry struck me until I thought back to the moment I last saw her. *"Could I have been wrong?"* I thought to myself. *"Was she ok?"* I replayed the moment over in my head. I remembered the blood. Her still body. Her eyes. She was so lifeless. So empty. The voice couldn't have been real.

In what felt like a brief moment, Mark had already disappeared in the darkness. His panicked shouts clouded his footsteps. "Mark!" I yelled. My calls out to him blended with the sounds of the screaming voice of Mrs. Cunningham and his replies to her. I ran as fast as I could through the catacombs, trying to follow the echoes of the voices. "It's not real, Mark!" I shouted between breaths.

"I'm coming, Pamala!" Mark hollered from a distance. "Mark, please! Help me!" the voice screamed. My attempts to get Mark's attention fell short and he ran after the voice. "Mark, stop!" I yelled again, trying to win over his sense. The shrieks seemed to get farther away from me. I picked up speed the best I could, but it didn't help. The voices turned to echoes. "Mark!" I shouted into the open cave as loud as I could manage with the breath left in me. I tried to listen but could not make out much through my labored gasps for air.

Right when I was passing between an opening into one of the empty spaces, shadows grew from either side of the passage in front of me. Two demons snapped their head around the corner toward me. Their grins dripped saliva through them and spilled onto the dusty ground. They trained their eyes on me as they slithered the rest of their tall bodies out from hiding.

"Boy of Midland." They said in unison. "We shall pour your blood over our offspring and molest your bones!" They approached me slowly, taking steps together like a reflection of each other. I backed away, tripping over myself and onto the floor of the cave. They cherished every moment of fear I gave them. I tried to get back up, but my legs rebelled. Their scratchy breathing filled their chest, getting louder and louder.

They were only a few feet away from me when my stomach began to rumble. The monsters started to chuckle until they saw the color of my eyes change in front of them. They froze as I rose into the air. Fear traded places, leaving my face, and sparking on theirs. Their cowering was a sound I had never heard before. The gasps took over the space around us. I felt tall. My legs became firm but still felt like they flowed with the liquid within them. The demons, once anxious to reach me, were now taking steps backward.

Each blast from within me disassembled the beings more. I towered over them as I watched their gruesome bodies become nothingness. Screams of pain from the distance caught my attention as I returned to normal. I ran toward it as fast as I could, managing to focus on only what was in front of me. The cave was redundant. I followed what would seem to be a path if there was one.

My heart was racing. I could not mentally keep up with what was going on. I had to take each minute, each moment, one by one. Shrieks that seem to surround me came and gone, distracting my focus. But I pressed on, moving as fast as I could through the cave. I was beginning to think I would be running forever until I heard a slight buzz in the distance. The noise sounded like a fly or bee in and out of the spaces of my breathing. I trained my ear to the sound. It was in and out, without rhyme. I followed it. I went through room after room, the sound getting a bit louder with each step.

Eventually, I started to see blurts of light reflecting off the walls in the darkness. I was finally able to make out the sound. Electricity. I ran after the sound and the light, grateful to have finally found a way that seemed to be hopeful. The sizzle of the buzz became sharper and more direct. Sounds of popping were more evident. The light helped show the way to what was in front of me.

As I got closer, I questioned what it could be. A burning stench scrunched my nose and kept getting worse and worse. I paced my movements to catch my breath quicker. The sudden and sporadic popping was now a bit hurtful to my ears. As I kept walking, the sound of wetness formed under me. I looked down to see some of the ground darker than the rest trailing up in front of me. A flicker of light lit the area up for a moment and realized the water I was stepping in was red.

I hurried towards the end of the trail, using the flickering light to guide my steps. The burning smell suffocated me as I picked up speed. Suddenly, I got to the end of the stream of the liquid. A shadowed figure rested stiffly on a pole that had been stuck into the ground of the cave. The image halted me. After a moment, I took a deep breath and eased closer to the figure. Before I could take another step, the sound of electricity rang through the walls. A flash of light from the pole's forks illuminated the area I stood in for a brief moment. Then I realize the figure wasn't a shadow.

It was Morris.

CHAPTER 23

"Love is something you can't teach. Something you can't be trained on. It is something no one truly knows how to explain, yet we are expected to exhibit it in a way that is flawless and unmarred. The smallest chip in a mindset can change the deepest hate into a love that can change the world. The opposite is true, as well. The fact that people die due to hate means that someone loves what they stood for so much, they murdered for it. Are they to be punished for loving, just because you love something else? For loving in an alternative method. If love and

*love alone is the answer, why does it create so many
questions?"*

//

Morris' impaled body hung lifeless from the
forks of the electric trident, like fruit from a tree. His
eyes pried open. The look of shock was still on his
face. The smell of charred flesh permeated the area's
air. Blood dripped from his body, down the staff of
the weapon, and onto the floor. I tried to step out of
it, but the damp ground was covered.

Horror coursed through me. Anguish.
Despair. Tragedy's grip held me hostage. I couldn't
breathe. Every breath, every whiff of his burnt skin,
felt like life and sanity leaving my body. I threw up
onto the blood-soaked floor in front of me. I sank
down by the wall next to Morris and began to sob.

My crying grew more uncontrollable every
second. More than I have ever let myself cry before.
The sparks and flashes of light from above me sent
me back into pain every few moments. I clenched my

chest as my heart felt like it was about to burst. Heat rushed over me. The crying started again as soon I thought it would stop. Over and over until I laid empty.

"Would you shut up already? I'm trying to read," a voice said at the end of the newly discovered hall. It summoned every bit of my attention. I get to my feet, holding on to the wall to stay balanced. My pants stuck to my shins with blood and vomit. I moved down the hall and peered around the corner.

A woman of average height and build stood at the far end of the vast area. Her pale skin looked sickly and washed. The straight black hair rained from under the long brim of her dark hat and draped onto her black dress. She was the first normal-looking thing I had seen in the caves besides Me, Morris, and Mark. The sight was shocking and underwhelming all at the same time.

The woman was reading the book. Behind her, Mark laid stiff on the ground. I walked in and she slowly moved their eyes from the pages to me. She was new to me but her corrupt smile looked all too familiar. She examined me, registering everything as she looked me over and returned her eyes to the book. "*You're* the Boy of Midland?" the woman said, chuckling. "You're a lot fatter than I imagined. Don't worry, your friend is still alive. For now." A deep breath escaped my lungs. She continued to read. I felt powerless. Exhausted.

"You truly have horrible friends," the woman mocked. I looked over at Mark's unconscious body, then Morris' lifeless corpse. Tears welled back up in my eyes. "Who are you? What did you do to him?" I croaked. The woman ignored me for a moment but then spoke up in a calm voice that somehow still cut like daggers. "Me? You did this," she countered with a smile.

My heart heated up. I clenched my fist until my hands hurt. I notice my breathing picking up, in tempo with my rumbling heart. "Relax, boy," the woman said. "I'm called Drea. And I come bearing good news. You can fix absolutely *everything*." She closed the book, causing it to whimper, and placed a finger in between the pages she was reading. I backed away as she tried to approach me. She noticed my fear and stopped, looking me up and down once more.

"I can't believe you're the one causing all this trouble," Drea expressed with a look of disappointment. The look of surprise on her face seemed to be genuine. It hurt more than the words themselves. I noticed the book trembling in her long pale arms. She stiffened me with her eyes. Her beauty was blurred by the evil in her gaze. "I can make all this go away," she offered. "The pain. The chasing. Aren't you tired?" I didn't answer. I didn't want to admit how worn out I was. How much these last few days had stripped me of every bit of reality and sanity. I tried to stare back blankly, but I was sure how I felt was evident.

"What's going on?" I blurted finally. "Tell me!"

"You are the one that has to end this, Boy of Midland," Drea stated.

She straightened up and pointed at me. "You are the one who partook in the ceremony, instead of

Stellan's servant, as intended! You are the one that has hindered Stellan from what is deserved! What belongs to us!" I began to notice how hot I was as a single bead of sweat trailed down my face, escaping my temple and slithering down the side of my face. My legs quivered underneath me, but I managed to keep my balance somehow.

"Ever since you robbed Stellan of the fruit's power, you have halted everyone else from offering life to Stellan. You have *taken* from us!" Drea's voice began to get deeper and louder. The words gave me the chills. She took a moment to compose herself. Straightening out the brim of her hat, she continued.

"But you can make it right," Drea said, her tone sizzling into a murmur. She opened the book back up and drew her finger over the page she was on. "You need to make it right."

"Make *what* right?" I snapped. The words came out airy and broken.

"You need to finish the ritual!"

The book shrieked at Drea's sudden volume. She struck the cover of the book as hard as she could, sending a brief wail out from it. The sound from the hit rippled around us into the walls. Drea recuperated once more. "You are the one that must say it." I was puzzled for a moment, then realized what she meant. My heart was beating a hundred miles per hour but all I could think about was Mark, Morris, and Mrs. Cunningham. I couldn't shake the thought of them being dead because of me. All to help me get out of this. It was my fault. And Nikki. Genie. Now that these things knew who I was, they would never be safe.

"I will say whatever you want if it brings my friends back and keeps my family safe," I declared.

"Very well…" Drea replied, grinning.

"But I don't trust you. Give me the book."

"The book belongs to Stellan!"

The roar was harsh and telling, recoiling me back into the fear I almost strayed away from. She seemed to recognize that I closed back off. "The book belongs to the Almighty Stellan, but I will *tell* you what you need to say." Her growl faded into her original hiss. I paused. The hesitance frustrated her, but she remained as calm as she could.

"You need to make it right," she said, narrowing her eyes on me. I could almost feel her eyes trace my body. "Make it right, Boy of Midland," she said. Her stare didn't budge. The thought of what she could do to me paralyzed me completely. I couldn't even speak. Time seemed to stop as she said the words. Even the air around us felt motionless. For a moment, only the sound of popping electricity could be heard. There was no other choice. I broke the seal in my throat.

"What would you want me to say?" I submitted.

"Simply say, *Ninaunga mkono giza na kukataa nuru. Ninatoa nguvu zangu kwenye giza,*" Drea replied.

The words flowed from her mouth like silk. They were practiced and precise. "What if I don't say them?" I asked. Drea looked at me in disgust.

"What?" She barked. Her words rumbled around us. I felt as though she was surrounding me.

"What happens if I don't do this?" I tried again, pushing past my fear.

"I will destroy you and the ones you claim you love!" Drea hissed.

"You can't," I pondered. The realization and the words arrived at the same time.

"What?" Drea's bark rumbled again but had less of an effect.

"If you kill me, you don't get what you need. Or else you would have done it already."

I smiled at the thought, but quickly remembered that I may be wrong somehow. Drea's anger slowly molded into a cautious sneer.

"You don't know what the hell you're talking about!" she exclaimed.

"If you could kill me right now, I would be dead. You need me to say the words to turn things back to how they were before for you and the rest of those things that have been chasing me. They weren't ever trying to kill me. They were going to *capture* me! To force me to say that stuff from the book!"

My voice lifted with surety as I put the pieces together. The water within me began to flow, ready to emerge. Drea stammered to maintain the perceived dominance she once had. The understanding must have been evident in my face. She began to walk towards me. "Stay back!" I shouted. The words froze her. The shift made me realize how quiet I had been the whole time. I took a step towards the woman but stopped before it felt unsafe. "I want everyone back, or else I'm not doing anything for you or the rest of your dumb ass friends!" I demanded.

Drea slowly softened her expression to what she could shape into a sympathetic gaze. She grabbed her hands and placed them in front of her almost as if she was trying to seem humane. Relatable or comforting. "Little one," she said concerningly. "It must be hard for you, baby. I know you're hurting. You have been through a lot." She tilted her head and shook it softly, seeming as though she genuinely pitied me. I felt myself get less tense.

"You don't deserve any more heartache and misfortune," Drea said. She scoffed at the thought. "You didn't ask for anything of this. If your mother and father didn't want you, why did they have you? They dragged you here, just to mistreat you and leave you stranded in this toxic world alone. Now you're in all this mess and where are they? Gone. As always. Living their lives, happy that you aren't in it. What was the point?"

My eyes welled up. Her words were true. She was saying things I had been struggling with since I could remember. Hearing someone else validate my thoughts, really truly understanding what I was going through, was refreshing. Drea continued before I could respond. "And those *idiots* in your classes at school. If they only knew how remarkable you are. How much power you have inside of you. They would never want to bother you again. If they weren't so stupid, they would see. I would do anything for them to see. I wish there was a way they could understand what you are dealing with."

I broke down. I tried to keep myself focused, but I couldn't. There was so much pain pent-up in me. There was nothing I could do to keep from weeping. I covered my face in embarrassment. The tide inside me calmed. I couldn't stand to be seen like that. My body got hot from the emotion flowing through me.

I heard Drea approaching me, but I had given up. I didn't care what happened anymore. The people I loved were dead and it was my fault. I had no one to go to. I was weary. In pain. The thoughts weighed heavier on me with each moment. *"What was I going to tell Morris' parents? What was I going to do for Mark?"* The pressure of it all was unbearable.

Drea came over to me. She placed the book down on the floor next to her and embraced me. She placed her hand on the back of my head and cradled my head on her shoulder. The feeling sent me deeper into despair. Her hands carefully rubbed my back. Her touch was gentle and caring. Like that of what a good mother seemed like on movies or television.

"Oh, little one," she whispered. The words coated my body in warmth. After a little while, she slowly separated from me, sliding down her hand from my head to my neck. Her hands were warm, but chills coursed over my entire body. She looked at me with a look that I've only gotten before from Mrs. Cunningham. Drea gave me a gentle smile and rubbed her thumb back and forth across my teary cheeks.

"I want this over too," Drea reasoned, looking at me with gentle eyes. "I was sent here to get this over with for the both of us. He just wants this done." She smiled and I felt myself trying not to. "You got put into this and I'm just trying to get you out and get things back to normal," she continued. "Wouldn't you fight for *your* friends?" It felt as if I was talking to someone else. Her large brim cast a shadow over my face, but I could still tell she was looking at me.

Drea picked up the book from the cave floor and stood close to me. "We can deal with all those people that hurt you, little one," she said. "You won't have to worry about anyone bothering you ever again. But we can only do that if you help me, ok?" I stood still for a moment contemplating what she could mean, but not for long. I spent so many years with things being hard. I just wanted, for once, to be at peace. "Ok," I said, nodding in response. "I'll do it." Drea smiled. I smiled back that time.

CHAPTER 24

"People say love is blind. But how do they know? If they see it, does that mean they hate? What made love blind? Was it its naivety? Or did it love so much, it didn't care about what was going to happen to it? Are we all to be blind? Pouring ourselves out onto one another without looking for reciprocation? Without wanting truth? Is love meant to be led by something or someone else? Or is blindness in and of itself the sight we need to move forward with its purpose? The only thing to be feared is love. The love

of despair. The love of comfort. The love of evil. If love is blind, hate has vision."

//

Drea didn't seem so bad after all. There was a pleasant twist in her voice that I missed before. She stood there still, looking at me as if I was a son of her's that she wanted to help through a hard time. The thought of getting everything back to normal, minus the pain I had to deal with for so long, blanketed me with peace. Soothed me. It was almost euphoric. I was grateful for an opportunity to fix things. My mind raced with all the calmness that was to come. I was sick of being made fun of. Sick of getting beat. Sick of hurting in every way possible. I'd do anything to make life better. No one had ever made things better. Until now.

"Are you ready?" Drea asked. She stood quietly watching me as I thought about what was to come. I nodded and she smiled. "Hold out your hands, like you're offering something to someone." I lifted my hands and turned my palms upward. Drea motioned for me to put my hands together. I slowly brought my hands closer to each other, forming what looked like a cup with my hands. She nodded in acceptance.

My heart was racing, but I wasn't exactly sure why. I noticed the sweat starting on my forehead. "I need you to say these words very carefully." Drea seemed to be more serious now. I could feel my throat dry up.

"Okay, wait! I hesitated. She fended off an irritated look and forced a smile.

"Yes?" she asked somewhat impatiently.

"After this, after I say what you want me to say, what will you do to the people who hurt me?" I asked.

"What do you *want* me to do to them?" Drea replied.

"I don't know. Just… I don't know. Just don't kill anyone for me."

The request felt manufactured. Foreign. I couldn't say I cared about the people, including my mom, but I didn't want anyone to die. I may have wanted to kill them sometimes, but I didn't want them dead. Drea looked at me puzzled. "You want to spare the ones that have hurt you, boy? They've done so much to you. After giving you the existence you have, you still want them alive?" Her surety in her questioning made me question my request. I nodded my head, a little confused myself. She didn't grant me a response but prepared to give me the words again.

"One more thing!" I hurled out. This time, she was less willing to withhold her anger.

"What *is* it?" she barked.

"Are we going to get out of here? What happens after all this?"

Drea blurted her reply abruptly, seemingly discarding the warm loving character she played just a few minutes ago.

"This place is for wars that can't be had in your world. It is part of… nevermind. That is not a concern at the moment. An exit will be granted once this is done," she replied.

Drea's answer seemed to have come out faster and with less of a filter than she meant them to. "We don't have time for more questions. We must end this!" I raised my hands up again, as they have drooped down from where they were before. "Carefully." She reminded me again. Her eyes reverted to the thin narrow eyes I first saw her with. I nodded with understanding. She searched the book for a page she needed it open to and stood next to me. The shadow of her large hat covered the page but I listened closely to follow along.

"Ninaunga mkono -" Drea said.

"Ninaunga mkono," I repeated cautiously.

"Giza na,"

"Giza na,"

"Kukataa nuru," The book began to tremble in her hands.

"Kukataa n-"

Suddenly, I heard the faint sound of grumbling. The bit of commotion caught the attention of Drea also. The sound approached us from behind. "Braxton…" the voice murmured. It was Mark. Drea growled. "Braxton, get away from her. She's a witch," Mark grumbled, staggering to his feet. Drea raced toward him. She was almost to him before I could even face her direction. Before I could do anything, I heard the impact of Drea's fist hitting the wall behind him. The book fell from Drea's hand and tumbled down to the floor.

Mark had dodged her blow by barely an inch. Drea stood up straight, putting her hat back in place. "I knew I should have killed you," she said to Mark with a sinister tone. I ran over to Drea, who prepared to swing at Mark again. She moved so quickly, it was like a blur. She tried to punch him, but that time I was ready for her. I pushed Mark out of the way and hit Drea in the mouth.

I pulled Mark away, putting distance between us and Drea. She wiped the blood from her lip and smiled at the sight of it. It was a deep black and smelled like rotten eggs. I reached my arm out to protect Mark. I motioned for him to run toward the hall. "Mark, I know what to do now to end all this!" I shouted. But he wasn't paying attention. He pushed me out of the way right as Drea came down with a kick that cracked the ground underneath us.

I fell to the ground but quickly stood to my feet. "Wait, we can fix everything!" I shouted to Drea. I looked over right as Mark was running toward the book. "Braxton, I can't let you do anything she says!" Mark hollered. I stopped, confused. "But I can stop this," I advised. "She told me-" Before I could finish explaining myself, Drea's hat flew above Mark's head. Just as the shadow of the hat was passing over him, a bolt of lightning came from inside of it, electrocuting him. He fell to one knee and tried to hold himself up. He let out a howl as the pain went through him.

Before he could get up from the shock, Drea came running up and kicked him to the ground. He rolled for a couple of feet from the hit. The top of her head was white all the way around. The skin on her head was crispy and pale. Drea reached out her hand and her hat returned to her grasp. She threw it again towards Mark but he managed to roll out of the way just in time to miss the 2nd bolt.

I didn't have time to think. I ran over to Drea at full speed and punched Drea as hard as I could. She flew back several feet and banged against the wall before rolling on the ground. She got up and looked down the nearby hallway. A look of satisfaction covered her face. She started to make her way down the entrance.

I hovered in the air above her and dropped to smash her under my heels, but she dodged it. I backed up from the fight and noticed out of the corner of my eye that Mark reached the book. I ran over to him. "You've got to stop her! She is tricking you somehow!" Mark exclaimed. I looked at him with anger in my eyes. "Listen!" I barked at him. "She was telling me something to say to help everyone! I can bring everyone back!" My words fell to the ground as Drea came back from the hall to continue the fight. She was holding the electric trident that was pierced through Morris' body.

I screamed at Drea to listen to me, but she seemed to ignore me. I tried to think of something, anything to say that could help. "Drea, I'm ready to say the words, but I can't let you hurt him!" I pleaded. Drea came towards Mark with her trident aimed towards him. We moved out of the way right as the trident pierced through the ground between us. I ran over to Drea and delivered another punch. The impact sent her head backward. I tried to hit her again but she caught on and moved. Her movements were quick. She struck back, knocking me in the eye. I flinched but caught her fist and blasted her with my other hand. She rolled away as the pulse hit her.

"Braxton, are you ok?" Mark asked.

"Yea," I replied. "I mean no."

"I saw what she did to Morris. Braxton, I'm-"

"It's ok!" I interrupted. "I know how to get everyone back!"

"What?"

Mark's look of confusion and hope got me a bit nervous, but I continued.

"This lady! Her name's Drea! She told me I can say stuff to reverse everything, I just need to get to the book to finish the chant!"

"Pamela too?" he asked hopeful, widening his eyes at the thought.

"Yea, her too!" I exclaimed.

"What do you have to do?"

"I have to get the book and say something she found inside it! Once I say what she wants, everything goes back!"

"What exactly did she say when you were talking to her, Braxton?"

"She said if I said the stuff that she was telling me to, she would get rid of the people that hurt me and make everyone come back."

Mark froze. He looked down and away from me for a moment, thinking about what I was saying. "What are you thinking about?" I yelled. "What's the problem? I can fix all this! We can finally be done! I can finally have peace in my life!" Mark didn't say anything back. When he finally turned to me, he had tears in his eyes.

"Braxton, she's lying."

"No, she isn't!" I screamed. "You weren't there! You don't know!"

"She's lying, Braxton. She's a witch. She got me too using Pamela's voice. It was magic. Nothing down here can be trusted."

I took the book from his hands and started to walk away. I didn't want to deal with him anymore. "You'll see!" I shouted to him behind me.

CHAPTER 25

"I'm going to make things right."

//

I walked over to Drea with the book, ignoring all the cries from Mark. I didn't care. I was going to fix everything. I had to. It was my fault, and I was going to make it right. I opened the book and it began to tremble. It was whimpering and shaking. "It's ok," I said to it. "I'm gonna make it right." Mark ran towards me but, I ran away from him. "No!" I yelled. "This is my fight! I have to end this!"

Drea threw her hat again, but Mark moved out of the way right before the shadow cast over his left shoulder. The sound of the bolt jarred me for a minute, but I was able to stay on my feet. I ran farther from Mark, not protecting him any longer, turning the pages as fast as I could.

None of the words looked familiar to what Drea spoke before. I quickly flipped the pages, looking for anything close to what we were planning to say. Shouts from Mark peeked in and out of my hearing, but I was too focused on finding the page to pay attention to it. Mark ran back into the room.

"Braxton!" Mark yelled. I shook my head. "I have to find it. I have to make it right!" He ran closer to me, keeping his eye on Drea to stay safe. "Braxton, there's nothing you can do! They are gone! She was lying to you!" I ignored him. Drea crept closer to us, so we hurried to one of the safer corners of the area we were in. I barely took my eyes off the book. "Braxton!" Mark attempted again. I continued to skim the pages for any sign of the words from before. "Mark, I have to do this." He tried to reply but his voice was drowned out by my focus.

Then, out of nowhere, Drea rushed toward me, and I crashed into the nearby wall. The impact caused rubble to fall in the distance. I laid on the ground in pain. Sparks of electricity chased around my body. Drea's huffing got louder as she stood over me. Her hat was more tattered than before but still intact and laid crooked on her scarred head. The light from the electric trident pulsed stronger brighter the more she held it. Blood trickled down its prongs.

Drea's blood-covered face appeared tired. I could tell that she was completely exhausted. The black blood streaked down her cheek and onto her dirty dress. Nevertheless, she put on the best grin she could as she sauntered over to me. I tried to get up, but the electricity kept me from getting to my feet. Drea raised her trident. The electricity from her hands pulsed into it. "It looks like we'll have to just see what happens," she snarled.

"Wait!" I yelled. Drea stopped. She looked at me with the same look of disgust as before. "We have the book. And I can say the words. That's what I thought you wanted," I said, confused. Drea took a moment to catch her breath, exchanging glances between me and Mark. "I need the page with the words to finish what started all this. To make everything right," I pleaded.

Drea placed her hands lower on the staff of the trident and pointed it in my face. The tip of the longest prong was inches from my face. The light and buzzing made me flinch and recoil, but she didn't care. I held out the book for her to help me find the page. She took her other hand and flipped through the pages until she got to where she was before. Drea pressed her finger down on the page with enough force to make me almost drop the book. I could see her bloodshot eyes staring at me under her hat's brim. "Say it," she growled. Her dark blood dripped down her teeth and chin as she spat the words at me.

I looked down at the page. I saw the words and the picture of the hand gesture she wanted me to do before. "I can't remember them. How to say them, I mean," I confessed to Drea. She looked annoyed at me but knew I wasn't lying. She clenched her jaw and looked over at the page. I glanced at Mark, who stood back seemingly unsure of what to do. Although I couldn't make out much of his face, I could tell he was hurting. He had helped me so much. I didn't want anyone else to die.

"Could you not point that thing so close to my face?" I asked. Drea sneered at me angrily. She was becoming infuriated. "Just say *the words*, boy!" she replied. Her words injected fear in me worse than the look in her eyes did. "I will," I replied. "It's just that I am trying to bring people back and you are about to kill me. No one else is supposed to die" I choked on the words as they come out. They didn't make sense to me, but I meant it. I had rarely protected myself before.

Drea ground her teeth. The sound gave me chills. She sniffled a couple of times and took a labored breath. After looking down for a moment, she looked up at me with the most forced smile I had ever seen. She took a quick glance at Mark and then back at me. Drea placed her hand on the back of my neck and brought herself closer to me. I looked up at her taller frame. Her milky eyes, although beaten and faded, glowed through the shadow of her hat. They were softer than before. She gently rubbed my neck with her thumb. "Little one, I promise I will take care of everything as soon as-"

Suddenly Mark's voice burst in. "I see what you're doing!" He yelled. He quickly snatched the hat from Drea's head and tossed it away. "It's that hat!" he exposed. The shadow from the brim of the hat lifted and my eyes brightened. The colors in the room started to get brighter and the sounds around me got clearer. Drea let out a wail as she reached for her drifting hat. "Don't touch that, you bastard!" she squawked.

Then, I sprung up from the cave floor, maneuvered the trident from Drea, and threw it at her as hard as I could. The prongs went through Drea's abdomen and pinned her to the wall behind her. Black ooze seeped from her screaming body. The buzz and pops from the electric shock sound like small fireworks going off in the room. Drea gulped for air, grasping for every bit she could get, but only could gather enough for a few words.

"Brax-Braxton," Drea muttered, almost inaudibly.

"You lied to me," I replied. A tear started to streak down my face, but I wiped it away before I let her see it. She didn't deserve to.

"No. No, I didn't," Drea replied. She tried to stand straight the best she could, but her legs repeatedly slipped in the puddle of blood underneath her. "My words were, were *true*!"

"You had me under a spell!"

"The spell was only- to get you to listen!"

"I'm done with you," I declared, looking away from her to let her struggle alone.

"You can still make it right, Braxton. Sa- say the words, and you'll see."

I paused for a moment. The book was gripped in my hand ready for me to make a decision. Confusion and hopefulness and curiosity and heartache swirled around in me, not allowing for a single moment of clarity. I had the book. I found the words. *"What if she isn't wrong?"* I thought to myself. *"What if I can really make things the way they were?"*

I stroked the book with my thumb. I had to make a decision. It was all up to me. "Your friends died trying to help you with this. I can have them brought back. But not if you don't help me." I ignored Drea until she said the very next thing. "There's one more thing," she mentioned. I looked up at her diminishing body. "The powers you have. They aren't meant for you. They've been holding you together in an unnatural way. Your strength. The wisdom you have. They will be no more. You will surely perish. This world only creates an exit when a war has been concluded. This war… this doesn't end partially. To defeat me is to defeat yourself!"

From all the time Drea had spoken, she had not seemed surer of her words before. She looked at me, not with eyes of deceit, but with eyes of transparency.

"What are you saying?" I asked Drea.

"We ha-have weaponized the ancient ways," Drea replied.

"What do you mean?"

"You have received power from our doing. If you end this your way, you will have no more. You must relinquish everything you gained from us."

Mark took a step closer but stopped before he got too close to me. "I don't know about this, Braxton," he said with concern. I tried to take a deep breath, which didn't help at all. My heart grew heavier the longer I thought about Drea's words. If I gave her what she wanted, this could all be over, and I could finally live a life free from the pain I had grown accustomed to. But if I ended her, if I finished this, everyone would be safe from the Mijenta spell. But if I did that, who knew what would happen to me. I didn't deserve more hurt. But the lives of so many people that would probably hurt me anyway would be saved.

"Speak the words, Braxton," Drea begged. Her words grew harder for her to force out. "Say the words, baby, and everything will be ok. Make it right." My heart burned at the thought of their smiling faces. I don't know how I was supposed to go on without them. "Help me. He-help, me. Please." Drea's body was getting weaker by the moment. She had given up trying to stand and let the trident pinned in her hold her up. "They don't know, but *we* know, Braxton. They could never understand. Free me from this and we can bring your friends back to you."

The thought sounded so sweet. So much like salve on an aching wound. I missed Mrs. Cunningham and Morris so much. Also, I needed rest. I needed rest so bad. I look up at Drea, who is barely clinging on to existence. She looked at me with desperate hope. I placed the book on the floor and walk closer to her. She orchestrated a smile in the midst of all the pain she felt. Mark reached out for me, but I waved him away to stop him from interfering. "I have to do this," I said to him. "I have to make it right." Everything seemed to fade in the background as I got closer to Drea. "Thank you, Braxton," Drea cried, in a broken tone.

I grabbed the staff of the trident and drove it further into Drea's body. "No!" She screamed as the prongs slid in deeper. She tried to pull it out of her, but the ink-like blood slipped between her fingers and onto the floor of the cave. She blinked hard, trying to understand what was happening to her. Her frying flesh sizzled more and more with each passing second. After some time, her pale head dropped, spilling the charcoal blood from her mouth onto her lifeless body.

I backed away and stared at Drea. The lightning from the trident fizzed in and out like the sign of an old building. I wiped away the sprinkles of dark blood from my face and watched it slowly fade from my knuckles in sync with Drea. Mark walked over to me. I didn't see but I could feel him looking at me.

The book wiggled on the floor of the cave. The sound from it sounded like a child wanting to be picked up. I retrieved it from the floor and it flipped through the pages on its own until it got to the 2nd to the last page. The two pages I saw were blank. I tried to flip it to one of the ones before, thinking it made a mistake. But the book returned itself to the page it was on. It shook again. "What am I supposed to do?" I asked. Mark leaned over my shoulder to take a look at the page to try to help. He stopped once he saw they were blank.

Then the water from within me engulfed me. My eyes tinted to the familiar shade of blue that it had before. Power from my whole body moved into my hands and onto the pages of the book. I felt emptier than I had ever before. Sounds that seemed like crystals and xylophones rose gradually and filled the room. After a few moments, the blank pages of the book were filled with words. The letters were illuminated from the page. The left page had three horizontal lines in the center of the page. On the right page, there was a letter. It was in handwriting that was different than the rest of the book. It was clear and very legible. But what scared me the most was how it started.

To The Mighty & Meaningful Braxton,

THEN, A BOY

We thank you. Without your sacrifice, this world would be a place of turmoil and chaos. Only you could be trusted with the task of completing this part of the war for us. The heart you carry has been one we have been in search of for a long time. The pains you have felt along the way will not go in vain. The fruit of the tree you have eaten from will go on to replenish the world, and worlds, for many years to come. Take joy in the hardship you have faced. To The Mighty & Meaningful Braxton, we thank you.

You have one final task to complete your journey.

I looked over at Mark. "This book," I said, "this book knew my name!" Mark gazed at the pages in bewilderment. "Those pages are blank," he replied. Before I could respond to him, I noticed a new sentence appear on the page. I said the newly emerged words the best that I could.

"NARUDISHA NGUVU NILIYOTUMIA"

All of a sudden, my head started pounding. The first two lines on the left page filled in with someone else's crossed out name on the first line and my name on the line under it. My name slowly began to cross out. Right when the line got to the last letter of my name, the pain in my head got much worse. I dropped the book and grabbed my head in agony. I screamed for help. I felt Mark trying to pull me off of the ground, but I couldn't get up.

Cramps in my stomach came and got worse and worse. My body started to ache. All over. More and more until I was crying. I vomited from the pain. Then I felt my body curl up. My fingers became disfigured and bent in ways they have not been able to do before. Finally, my neck strained up and snapped to the left. I was on my side but saw upwards.

I saw the look of horror on Mark's face. He glanced behind him. A bright light came into the cave. I closed my eyes to block the shine, but I could still see the glow through my eyelids. Mark picked up me from the ground of the cave. I couldn't move my body at all. I could hear him telling me he was going to get me help. How I did such a good job. And how everything would be ok. I could hear the cries for help from Mark overhead. I could hear the screams from people in the distance. I could hear all the people around me. But all that seemed to come to mind was the pain.

EPILOGUE

Rumors of the murders of Pamela Cunningham and Morris Wilson spread quickly throughout Midland. The murders were soon followed by the sudden disappearances of numerous citizens of Midland, including Midland high school teacher Alfred Fredrickson and Midland Memorial Medical Center's chief of medicine Dr. Eric Coleman.

Some are led to believe the person responsible was Barbara Lee, a physical education teacher who reportedly went missing soon after the events. Others claim Mark Cunningham, the husband of Pamela Cunningham, was directly involved as he was the last to see the victims alive. While most of Midland's residents state the primary suspect is Braxton Tatum, whose quiet demeanor and stand-offish behavior reflect that of someone capable of such a crime.

The news traveled worldwide and was often referred to as The Braxton Tatum Murders. Court hearings went on in the city of Midland for many weeks. Officer Milton Berkley stated that Braxton fled the scene of an accident and could not be located for some time.

There were also reports of an abandoned vehicle left on the intersection of 19th Street and Kansas Ave where witnesses claim they saw Mark, Braxton, Pamela, and Morris driving recklessly, causing multiple accidents. The judge eventually decided that there was not enough substantial evidence to convict Mark or Braxton for the murders.

After the hearings, Mark left the city of Midland to return to his hometown in another state. A time of remembrance was declared for Pamela Cunningham at Midland High School, where students and staff members gathered together to acknowledge the teacher's life and the impact she had on the school. Many have stated that the crime is one that will stain Midland High forever and they hope that justice is served by the city of Midland convicting Braxton Tatum to life in prison. Some have even petitioned for capital punishment.

Meanwhile, Braxton Tatum became a resident in an assisted living facility on the outskirts of Midland. An unknown individual paid his expenses for all of the foreseeable future with a very large lump sum. Braxton spends his days in his wheelchair looking out of the room's large window.

Although visit attempts from news stations and television executives were initially plenty, visitation has simmered into very occasional and brief visits from Nicole "Nikki" Johnson and Eugene Barwell, Braxton's older and younger siblings, respectively. Braxton's inability to speak and distorted body posture has proven to be difficult for the family members to withstand.

Beyond the room checks from the members of staff for the facility, Braxton is primarily alone gazing out of his room's window, awaiting the one coming next. Next to Braxton's bed in a drawer is the book that has been with him through his journey. The book remains safe in his possession.

DEAR READER

I want to thank you for taking the time to read my first ever book. This story is very personal to me, and I am very proud of it. I relate deeply with a lot of the matters involved in the story. I am grateful for the opportunity to share this series with the world after multiple years of working on it.

More of the world is on the way. In the meantime, leaving a review would be extremely helpful for me. Word of mouth is beneficial as well. You can also purchase or stream the official score for Then, A Boy on all major music platforms.

Follow me on social media to stay up to date on my writing.

Shermanbmason.com
Twitter: @ShermanBMason
Instagram: @ShermanBMason

ACKNOWLEDGEMENT

After working on this for so long, I could spend a long while thanking people. Mostly the ones that kept from going insane during the process. Chiefly, my daughter Yolanda. I owe her my life. Many times over.

Thank you, Aarthi and Agsharah for reading my early draft and keeping me excited about this.

Thank you, Alisha for being the first person to ever tell me I was their favorite author.

Also, a bunch of other people. But I'm tired and need to order the proof copy to see what this looks like. Thank you for reading. Take care.

ABOUT THE AUTHOR

Sherman B. Mason is an author with experience in Young Adult, Horror, Science Fiction, Crime, and Fantasy. Sherman's works includes Errored Cherubs, Cruel Beyond, and No Weapon.

www.ingramcontent.com/pod-product-compliance
Lightning Source LLC
Chambersburg PA
CBHW030832110726
47900CB00006B/1851